OBURONI

AND OTHER STORIES

ANDREW REES

Oburoni and Other Stories
Copyright © 2023 by Andrew Rees

ISBN: 978-1962497039 (sc)
ISBN: 978-1962497046 (e)

The Reading Glass Books
(888) 420-3050
production@readingglassbooks.com

Table of Contents

FOREWORD

These short stories were written during my recent stay in Ghana, hence the title 'Oburoni' meaning 'white person' in Twi, a word I often heard when greeted in the streets, especially by children. Oburonis are relatively rare in Ghana. It's a word that symbolises the sense of being different, but at the same time, the sense of being welcomed and accepted. It evokes fond memories, a reminder of one's individuality, and so becomes a fitting title for this book and its first story. With its associated range of experiences, it sets the tone for the other stories which cover a number of themes such as family ties, adaptation, expertise, loss and strength. They include the frustration of finding work and coping with a difficult job, the importance of family, the dedication of an expert, and the suddenness of a tragic situation. The mixture of joy and sorrow, the highs and lows of life that we can all relate to, appears in different guises in several stories. Likewise the sense of searching that lies deep within the human condition. All surface in the different backgrounds of these twelve stories.

My thanks to Christine for diligent and thorough proof reading.

I have not intentionally modelled any story character on anyone I know.

For Angel, Michelle, Kharis, Chief and Andrew

OBURONI

'Oburoni!'

'Oburoni!'

The two children ran out from the front of their house, shouting and waving after him, repeating the cry as he walked along the dusty road to the store. He waved back, a greeting that seemed to encourage them, as they chorused together:

'Oburoni bye bye!'

John smiled inwardly. The feeling of natural warmth outweighed any strange reminder that he was a curiosity here. He turned the corner, nodding to acknowledge the greeting of a leisurely cyclist, before reaching the open doors of the kiosk, and asking for soap powder and bread. The folded five cedi note he handed over was exchanged for a crumpled red one and a small twenty pesewa coin. He ventured further, past a hen with her five tiny chicks, to see if the covered stall that sometimes sold bananas was occupied, but there was no one there. It was too early in the day. An older man sat opposite beside a pile of melons, but that was all. So, meandering his way round the huge puddles and soft mud of the road, John returned home the same way he had come, pausing to view new work on a half-built house along the way.

It was getting hot now in the early afternoon, over thirty degrees celsius, and he was glad to retreat to the shade of his room. Years ago his mother would have scolded him for staying indoors in fine warm weather, but it was different here, time to lie low and wait till late afternoon, an hour before dusk (invariably around 6.15pm), before venturing out again.

A soft knock at his door interrupted the quiet.

'Mr. John, Mr. John.'

He slid the bolt and opened the door. It was the caretaker with the drinks he had ordered, four cans of malt beer. John fumbled around for some money and paid him, before sinking into the sofa once again. The whir of the ceiling fan gave the room some coolness, while the curtain, covering the glass louvres, provided shade. This was his haven of calm, the fortress of home, his home in Ghana.

From time to time he paused for perspective on his life here. A thin, greying man in his late fifties, seemingly shuffled, like a spade in a pack of cards, to a place where no one would find him. He lived in a self-contained apartment at a hostel, a mile down an unmade road off a highway that was itself between towns, as immersed into local society as you could hope, a solo existence. Recognised by his skin, but then unrecognised for his past. No history of living here, just a recent arrival, his slate was wiped clean.

Why here, a long way from home, family, friends? The story was too long to tell. Shifts in living behaviour usually occur with a few years planning, but this had been more sudden, a reaction to being made redundant from his job in London, combined with his now ex-wife leaving and removing the children, both in their early teens, to her family home in Scotland. With the latter, devastation gave way to action, the need to clear and sell a house. And once that hurdle was jumped, the company merger at work was soon announced - weak utterances on job security giving way to the reorganisation announcements that meant only one thing. No one was indispensable, least of all John, and so within six months he had lost family, home and job.

Fifty seven years old, he had nowhere to go and nothing to do when he woke up in the morning. Well, until he made his own plan that is. He had sufficient financial independence, enough saved in his pension, so it was time perhaps to look further afield. A sudden vacuum had appeared in his life, which occasional visits north to see his children were not going to fill, nor the prospect of a new job. One day a father, a breadwinner, full of purpose, the next relieved of his responsibilities, his medals stripped off. It was time for something new.

He had always thought about doing something for community. Which community? It seemed a noble idea, and certainly more meaningful than being buried in the finance department of a head office, that had been his experience of the last ten years. He would need to do paid work again, for sure, but could try short-term contract work, rather than seek a permanent post. Meanwhile, if change meant change that might as well include change of location, indeed change of country or continent.

Africa, and teaching? John had no construction or medical skills. So digging wells or running clinics weren't his forte. But teaching? He had run specialist courses at work, though that was far removed from teaching six year olds how to read. He remembered his mother's experiences as a part-time English teacher. He had intentionally rebelled against that career and wanted to do something different. Maybe now the wheel had gone full circle and he could consider it. He made inquiries and emailed a major charity providing additional facilities in West African villages. Expression of interest led to firm dates and here he was, volunteering at a local private school at Kasoa, outside Accra in Ghana, doing anything from supervising sport to teaching Maths for an age range from seven to thirteen.

Day one living in a different culture, doing a different career, being a different person. Or was he? He was still the same old John Evans, with the infectious smile, and the trademark 'Come on you' comment when trying to evoke a response from anyone: son, salesman, shopkeeper or stranger. His unchangeable DNA was now resurfacing in a new environment, giving and receiving. And how they loved him. Young children greeted him a block away from the school gate, insisting on carrying his bag, asking him to take their class, as if he needed reminding. It was so nice to be wanted. The young ones, touching his arm, feeling the baggy skin of his elbow, looked into his eyes with happy, bright, wondrous faces.

Apart from the 'what will I be doing in thirty minutes time?' feeling on his first day, teaching had not been difficult. The syllabus was detailed enough to avoid any indecision over lesson planning, and class discipline you handled as required. Some teachers wielded and even applied the stick, but John was of milder mould, relying on voice tone to exercise

5

control over the children. They probably played him up more, but his view was that messing around in class was like shooting yourself in the foot. The pupil suffered from his or her self abuse, so best to let them learn that for themselves and quieten down. There was exuberance, yes, but no cynicism or wanting to fight the system. Lack of aptitude, yes, but generally not lack of attitude.

And so the daily routine took shape. Up at 6 am, walking the few dusty roads to arrive at school by 7.15 am, greeting everyone as he made his way to the office and prepared his lessons. Morning Assembly was held in the yard with prayers and the National Pledge, and the hand rung bell marked the start of lessons. Then, it was on with the school day, preparing, delivering, marking, resting. The 4pm Closing Assembly duly occurred, itself a precious moment where so many children would touch his hand or do a high five, so happy to make contact. Finally, he made the walk home, and did his daily shopping before the onset of darkness. There was comfort in its regularity and lack of intensity that somehow suited his time of life. Back in the UK he could have been contemplating retirement; here he was re-starting his work life.

It took a certain kind of person to do this. There were many periods of solitude, and sometimes too much time in his own company. It gave him space to reflect on the changes in his life. It had treated him unkindly, yes - he deserved better, but you had to adapt to circumstances. He saw anger over the breakup of his family as wasted energy. Nothing could be done about it, there was nothing to solve. What was done could not be undone, and they lacked for nothing with the money he sent back. The children were now in their teens and could make their own choices in a few years. At least he was online in Ghana and could make a video call with them each week. The mixing of blackboards and chalk here with smartphones and tablets was strange, the co-existence of old physical and new virtual spheres. In a place where he was as hidden from the world as he could be, John was still accessible, and an online social mixer where opportunity allowed. He was no recluse shutting the door on the outside world, despite his new life.

'Oburoni, my father is sick, we need two hundred cedis to pay the hospital. Please I beg you.'

This was Africa. Belief in God came from simple faith, unpolluted by the growing secularism of the West. Giving money for need was more a matter of being blessed by God than being repaid later by the receiver, as John had come to realise. Initially he had been generous, even with people he hardly knew, but was now much tighter given the sometimes incessant nature of the requests. Being white meant you had money. You might be here volunteering with no income, but it made no difference. You had to learn how to handle it and he was no bank. Money given out was rarely returned.

Often it was the more extreme variation, scamming, that put so many Europeans off the country. People trying to be smart with false names, photos, identities. Men posing as attractive girls behind the email barrier. John was sick of hearing about it. Yes he had some exposure from online dating, trying to fill the emptiness and have some fun, but realised he was getting nowhere. People here were so desperate to get money, so wanting a passport to a better life, and with so little chance of success. They would send clever forgeries to support requests for hospital fees. Trust was like gold dust, and precious in a way he had never imagined in the UK. Who could you trust? You needed a protective layer so as never to get hurt, never to get sucked in.

Then there were other situations…

'Oburoni do you like me?'

The young woman in the local shared taxi service was eyeing him, then holding his hand with a mischievous smile on her face, as she held her mobile phone in the other hand. It truly amazed him how many people had smartphones.

'You married?' She looked him in the eye.

After years of being married, it seemed strange for John to admit to his newfound single status, and he quite enjoyed saying no.

'Your number?' She asked invitingly. No preamble here.

Giving out a false number never worked as they phoned your mobile straight away to be sure contact was made. You could always ignore calls later on.

She placed her phone in his hand for him to type the digits. She rang him to check.

'I call you tonight.'

The soft voice and the smile made him curious. Invariably they would call, and he would engage in chat, but he never met up with them. It was amusing to play the game, motivated by money and security, not love. Women in their thirties happy to meet a 'mature' white man. John hadn't come here to look for a relationship. He had been bruised by experience. You never gave up interest, but at his age intimacy was becoming less important. Sharing his life with someone was still an aspiration though - how, if and when to be decided. It was not an expectation. Being white, male and single seemed stranger to Africans than being white and married. It made sense to them that there was someone with you to wash your clothes and cook your food. John managed the former himself, handwashing garments in the bucket before hanging them out to dry in the hot sun.

9

He took meals at the school: a filling lunch, especially the groundnut soup with fish and rice balls. The oily texture and deep salty taste of the soup was something to savour, quite delicious. At other times the smooth banku with telapia fish in a tomato sauce was uniquely local, even the way of eating it, breaking off small lumps of the doughy banku and dunking them in the sauce. He was glad to wash his fingers in a bowl of cold water afterwards. Eating in the evening was a varied affair for him, sometimes buying a pack of hot noodles, opening a can of sardines, or eating a hunk of bread with some tomatoes and avocado. John always kept the fridge full of the small bunched bananas, paw paw and pineapple sliced in a clear polythene bag. Fruit was plentiful. Green skinned oranges had been a curiosity at first but were not too dry. Large apples were expensive, probably imported, but he always ate them.

Fortunately, his health had held up, apart from occasional stomach spasms. The weekly malaria tablets, and heavy duty insect sprays on his bedding each night, did the trick. Then there was the bottled or sachet water bought everywhere that had never caused a problem. Often he took a sachet from the fridge, bit off the corner and enjoyed the feel of cool water cascading down his throat. Sweet nectar indeed. The sound of clapping and singing drifted his way from a nearby church.

Evangelical Christianity was a constant theme here, from big roadside posters advertising churches and their daily activities to radio testimonies, Bible verse stickers on car rear windows and even business names. John had no history of church involvement, but found it refreshing that people could be so open about their faith. By contrast everyone seemed guarded back home, expecting derision for their profession of faith, from the creeping paralysis of secularism. Religious 'correctness' masquerading as no religion, no convictions, a superiority of nothingness. It felt right to have faith in something more.

The tro tro, with the mate leaning out of the window hailing the destination, sped towards him and stopped.

'Circle, Circle.'

He stooped to get in and duly paid his three cedis to the mate. The large van stopped frequently, the door sliding to and fro as passengers embarked and then had to disembark to allow a person in the back row to get out. This was public transport in a country with almost no trains and relatively few local buses. You rarely had to wait. The driver quickly saw your hesitancy, and pulled over, just in case. So many tros, so many taxis. Accra traffic could be tediously slow, but pick the right time of day and you sped through.

For once he had an evening out, a visit for drinks at a bar near Mallam Junction, the big road divide where you worked out to which side of this great city you wanted to go. Left would take him on a main highway round the northern part of the city to Tema. Straight ahead, eventually, was the centre of Accra via the huge market at Kaneshie. He went left, and after another mile alighted from the tro, walking left past a row of shops. A recently met friend had introduced him to this bar, and, wanting something different, he decided to revisit it. He joined a group of five to whom he was quickly introduced. A large bottle of beer was placed in front of him.

The owner, Rose, came and sat next to him.

'Good to see you. How was your day?'

It had been a relaxing Saturday, a bit of a nothing day, but he had quite liked that - a break from the usual pressure to be doing something.

'Quiet, but that was fine. Did nothing really….'

'Chilled eh?'

The problem John had with chilling was that it brought up too much pain. He missed his children, and at times doing anything, to avoid thinking, seemed like an anaesthetic to handle that pain. Second or third best when you couldn't have the best. He had never doubted his commitment to Ghana. Coming here had been the right move. Anything nearer to home would have been too close to the memories of family life to handle well - maybe in a few years but not now.

'Planning to be here long?'

'Another hour or so,' he joked.

'You know what I mean,' she said smilingly.

He searched for an answer as he really didn't know how many more months he would be around. It was going well with the school right now, but anything could change.

'Rest of the year and take it from there.'

'What actually do you do?'

'Teach Primary Maths and ICT at a private school in Kasoa.'

'Oh wow, interesting.'

'Kids are great. Makes it all worthwhile.'

'I bet. What did you do in England?'

John explained his background as briefly as possible, not wanting to dwell on it. Sometimes he needed to remind himself of why he was here. It seemed a gamble in some respects. What would happen if one of his children wanted to come and live with him? He couldn't just drop everything and go home. Was it just going to be a year out, doing something different, or would he develop roots in Ghana? Too early to tell, yes, but then the question remained.

'Nice place here.' He change the subject.

'Yes, doing OK. It's taken a while to get it the way I want. Not the first place I've leased, but the best so far. Clientele are nice. Usually someone comes along each night. Could do with more people but taking the longer term view.'

John nodded. She meant that there were some bad days along the path. If he ever earned money here, it would be through owning something rather than being employed, as long as the school took his time. Then it was back to trust, who to manage your business, how to grow it. You couldn't do it on your own as a foreigner. Local help was everything.

He swallowed a mouthful of beer.

A chorus of laughter rang out from the group. He wished he knew enough Twi to join in, but as ever sat silently while they talked animatedly. He was a great believer in learning the local language, but age was blunting his principles and speaking English was always the easy option.

It was a good spot to watch the world go by, the traffic building as the evening progressed. A few others drifted in and sat at nearby tables. Rose moved over to look after them. John talked briefly to a man sitting nearby, but tiring, decided to drink up and go. He made his farewells.

The tros were full, so he took a taxi back, and even then sat in traffic, so that a forty five minute journey coming, took double that time going back. Once off the highway, the sandy, undulating surface of the road made for a bumpy ride, becoming worse, with water filled craters, the further they travelled. Once home, however, he sank into his sofa and thought to watch some TV before retiring. Ghana TV channels didn't interest him much, and signal was poor, but occasionally there was good movie, and so it was now. He saw it through, then retired.

Another day done, another dawn to anticipate, a long way from home. He smiled as he lay in bed. His life had changed completely over the last year. It was simpler, freer, and somehow more rewarding.

And anyway, where was his home now? He was warming to his new one.

FAMILY TIME

'Mum what's one thing we can never escape from?'

'Probably lots of things… our own body?'

'No you escape that when you die.'

'You escape a lot of things when you die.'

'Yes but this carries on without you.'

'Oh I don't know. You're being too cryptic.'

'Emit backwards. That's a clue.'

'Emit backwards? You mean instead of giving out something, we take something in?'

'NO! Spell EMIT backwards.'

'Oh I get it. Time.'

'Yes. Always there, but always unequal. Some are given twenty years, some eighty. Some waste their time, others are always busy doing something.'

'True. Something unequal that we never complain about, can never reverse or stop, and can never know the end for us. Invisible yet powerful.'

Cindy was relaxing in the living room with her teenage daughter Melissa. The teaser from the local paper was getting its anticipated reaction. She continued.

'Time heals they say, and time changes. I don't look any different today than yesterday, but take a photo of me today, and another in a year's time, and you instinctively know which is the older. We don't see change from day to day, but we do see it over a longer period. Strange. Sometimes you look younger, fitter, happier in a later photo than an earlier one.'

'Sometimes you age considerably more in one year than in another, for no obvious reason, like moving from childhood into teens, or hair turning from black to grey. Must be the hormones.' Melissa was in a reflective mood.

'It's stress. Today's stress can impact the body tomorrow, as if it needs time to absorb and react.

And some people don't show it even then. They're sixty years old looking like forty five.'

'Grow old gracefully. Have to try that....'

The doorbell rang interrupting their conversation. It was a charity collector, who gratefully accepted a £2 donation.

'Time heals too. You're hurting from something, but each day you feel differently about it, and the longer away from it the less the impact, like it doesn't matter anymore. You have to forgive.' Cindy drew on her experience of mental scars she had borne over the years.

'Or is it the heart and mind that heal like the body, and time just happens to be there?' Melissa was sharp.

'Yes, well put, it's not just time. Time is dimensional, not animate. It can't feel,' agreed Cindy.

'We're getting too deep now. Better stop.'

'What are you two talking about?' Kevin, Cindy's husband, entered the room looking for the TV Guide.

'Time,' replied Melissa.

'Time you stopped talking and put a cup of tea on, if you ask me.'

They all laughed.

'Stop,' said Nicky. 'Nice scene, Sunday afternoon in the living room, everyone reflective after a nice slow lunch.'

'But it's going nowhere,' she continued, 'you need to develop a plot. Time can be a theme but you need a story around it. Melissa has to do something, not just sit there making intellectual comments.'

'OK,' said Stephanie 'You're right, I'm writing the introduction with no idea where I'm taking the story.'

'Time is also too vague. It's implied in many stories. You need something more. Make something happen. You're building your characters, now develop them. It doesn't have to be dramatic, just interesting.' Nicky was thinking hard.

'I know.... a TV quiz!' Stephanie exclaimed.

'Ye... es, could work. Mother versus daughter. Competitive urge. Then Dad comes in with an answer that neither of them knows, the gestation period of a female elephant perhaps.'

'So the moral is that whoever comes top doesn't know everything. The history wiz coming a cropper on a science question.'

'Possibly...' remarked Nicky. 'The quiz gets better answers at home than in the studio. It gradually becomes a domestic quiz up and down the country, more than a contest between two TV panels. Father versus son, mother against daughter. So your theme might be how something intended one way develops into something else, bigger and better. Like the inventor of the mobile phone could never see the many uses to which it is now put.'

'OK, sounds good. I get you. Will think about it.' Stephanie promised.

'Competitive writing to match the competitive instincts. Adversarial. Winners and losers. That's what hooks a reader. The final tie-break question becomes more important than the winning goal in a football cup final.' Nicky was reinforcing the point.

'Or, even better,' she continued, 'write about family time. Families spend precious little time together. Online society and all that. Here we have Cindy, Kevin and Melissa together in the same room on a Sunday afternoon. They watch a TV show, movie, even a quiz together, enjoying each other's company. Later, Melissa has to do schoolwork, Kevin has to fix something, Cindy has to prepare dinner. Each go their separate ways. Family time over for another week.'

'Yes, good thinking Nicky.'

'Or yet again, the online society. Melissa just sits there with her phone taking messages all afternoon interrupting family time. Physically there with her parents, mentally out and about with friends or boyfriend. But that theme has been done to death methinks. We just accept all that now.'

Stephanie was deep in thought She had written a few short stories, seen them published in magazines, and enjoyed being favourably received. But she was running low on inspiration, and needed to meet other writers such as Nicky Black, herself a contemporary novelist. Showing samples of her work was a good way to get advice. She also had ambitions to write a full novel. Ideas were gradually forming but there were gaps to fill. That could wait. She wanted to continue the short stories for now, continuing her passion for originality such as was shown with 'Hidden Depths', her first effort.

Cindy brought in a tray bearing a full teapot, three cups and saucers, and a plate of biscuits.

'Afternoon tea served.'

She placed the cups and poured the tea. It seemed a nice change to use a tea service instead of kitchen mugs. Something done all too rarely.

'So what did you discover about time? Other than the time it takes to talk about it,' asked Kevin.

'Very smart Dad. It's a cryptic teaser out of the local paper. Something we can't escape from.'

'Or don't really want to escape from. Who cares about time? Doesn't hurt anybody.'

'You would if you weren't free. Doing time in jail. Wishing you were outside,' said Melissa.

'Well yes, suppose so. Freedom is more important.'

'Talking of time, it's four o'clock. 'Family Know How' is on. Semi-final if I remember. Let's watch,' suggested Cindy.

'Yes good idea,' Kevin and Melissa agreed.

The Taylor family of Harrow, parents and two teenage daughters, were pitted against the Gillmans from Bristol, with a teenage daughter and son.

They fielded some easy questions to start, settling the nerves. Then came the first tough one.

'What is the next perfect number after 6?'

'Perfect number, what's that?' Kevin was stumped.

'No idea. Maybe a number ending in zero, like 10?' said Cindy.

'So round numbers look perfect, like 100?' asked Kevin.

'No it's not. I should know this,' Melissa was struggling. 'Something to do with the number of ways you can divide it. Like 6 is 3 times 2, and also 6 times 1. Hang on… yes, you add 3, 2 and 1 (ignoring the 6) to get 6. But the next one, who knows… I'll guess 24.'

'Sounds good to me, but you'd need a computer to work it all out. These guys have got thirty seconds,' remarked Kevin.

The Taylor and Gillman families hadn't a clue. The answer was 28. Melissa had the right logic but the wrong answer.

'Close!' exclaimed Melissa.

There was then a section on sport, in which Kevin, as a keen follower of most sports, was able to excel, answering anything on golf, tennis, football, rugby and cricket.

Then followed geography. 'How many African countries start with the letter B?'

'Let's see,' said Cindy, 'Botswana, Burundi, that's two.'

'Can't think of any others,' commented Melissa, 'but geography was never my strong subject.'

'Benin. Makes three.' Kevin added, 'I think that's it.' The Taylor family seemed to agree.

'Need a new atlas. Some of these countries have changed names,' said Kevin.

The answer was four, Burkina Faso being the fourth.

'We're not doing so well here,' commented Cindy, 'pull your socks up team!'

The panel scores were close, and rounds on music and TV were keenly contested. First to the buzzer was the key, with penalties for wrong answers. Two points separated the teams moving into the history round.

'In the last 150 years, how many years has Britain had a king?'

'Not many,' said Kevin. 'When did Victoria die?'

'1900 or 1901, I think... mum do you know?'

'Present queen is from 1952, so I guess it's 51 years.'

Which was the right answer.

'Yay,' cried Melissa, 'success at last!'

'Queens hang around a long time. Was there ever a queen who had a short reign?' asked Kevin.

'Can't remember. We get fewer of them so they have to last longer,' remarked Cindy.

Two more rounds saw the Taylor family retain their narrow lead to win the match. A few more tough questions were too much for the three viewers, happy enough now to sit back, in contrast to earlier matches, when they participated and scored better.

'You'd have to know a lot to appear on that show,' reflected Cindy. 'Not for us I think. We'll stick to the armchair. Too nerve wracking in front of a camera.'

'Seconded,' replied Kevin. 'You either know the answer or you don't. Guessing doesn't work.'

'We tried,' said Melissa. 'At least we know when the pyramids were built now.'

Cindy cleared the tea cups away. It was time to walk the dog.

UNCLE BOB'S VISIT

Jill slit open the letter. A quick read led to a burst of joy.

'Ooooh! Uncle Bob. Coming to the UK. First time in over forty years.'

Dave looked up.

'Staying here?'

'Yes, well who else does he know? He can have the spare room. Haven't seen him for years. Last time... oh yes, I remember, Mum was still alive.'

'How long is he coming for?'

'Doesn't say... Oh yes, here it is. He thinks three months. Wants to see Stonehenge and Cornwall.'

'Well that shouldn't be hard to manage, but three months is a long time.'

'Come on Dave, he's my uncle. I'm sure he won't want to be staying here all that time. It's his first big trip anywhere since Marjorie died. That was over two years ago.'

'Typical Aussie… he'll want a country pub and plenty of sport to watch. A six pack of beer and a 40 inch flatscreen TV.'

'You're probably right,' commented Jill. 'They all dream about green grass, Devonshire teas, and village cricket matches. The quintessential England. Guess we can take him to a few places. Should take some time off to show him around.'

'Hmmmm. Not sure how much leave I can take. When's he coming?'

'July. We've got two months. I'm sure he'll fit in fine. He's in his early seventies. Not like we're inviting a couple of rowdy teenagers, worrying about what time they're coming home.'

'No, he's a creature of habit, I'm sure. Will be nice for him to have some company. Death of a wife is life changing. Living on your own, retired, can be really hard.'

'Yes sure,' agreed Jill. 'Let's face it, there's not much chance of us going to Australia in the near future.'

With a month to go, Dave was having misgivings. Three months was, after all, a long time to entertain someone. Even three weeks could be an eternity. Apart from going to see his friend in Cornwall, there was little chance Bob would venture far.

'I know he's family, Jill, but three months... It's a long time. Couldn't you have told him we can only have him for a few weeks?'

'Dave, he's my family. What am I supposed to do, discourage him? Tell him to book into the hotel down the road? Yes, I also think it's a bit long. Maybe he'll change his mind, but I don't want to make him feel we're unwilling to look after him.'

'You know what I mean. Set the expectations.'

'Well I'm not sure I do,' replied Jill. 'What actually are you asking me to do?'

'Just tell him we're away for part of the time. We need our privacy too. What about our week in Bournemouth?'

'Would you say that to your blood relative?'

'If I had to, yes.'

'Look Dave, he's coming all this way. The least we can do is welcome him. The time will go quickly. He'll want to do some touring which takes time out. You just have to be patient.'

'Hmmmm.'

'Oh what is this, husband versus uncle?' exclaimed Jill, storming out of the room.

There was a week to go before Bob's flight landed at Heathrow Airport.

For Dave, whatever view you took, this wasn't going to be fun. Rearranging holiday, clearing out boxes from the spare room, trying to make small talk with an Antipodean relative, none of it appealed. Maybe the best thing was to leave early for work and return late, giving over the house to Jill and her uncle. Slide in the back door at 9pm after a few drinks on the way home, and have a late coffee with them to avoid impoliteness, and keep the marital bliss.

After a long argument, they had decided to defer their week away until mid-August. Dave felt he was conceding too much. July was his long awaited holiday month, so why lose it. Jill had been happy to cancel it completely, but was persuaded to believe that Bob by then could manage on his own for a week - a compromise that suited neither.

Then there was a continuing discussion on where to take Bob, in the belief that he liked the great outdoors. Trips to the Chilterns, Oxford and the Norfolk coast were suggested, modified, and re-discussed - the usual planning for when an overseas visitor arrives.

Jill was gradually getting excited about the impending arrival. Her only memories of Uncle Bob went back to a family tea party in her teens when he was last over to visit many years ago. He was born and bred Australian, from country New South Wales. His father had moved out to Sydney from London at the time of the Depression, initially settling in the city and then meeting a girl from Bowral, further south, and settling there. Bob was born just after the war, and lived there till he was eighteen, before moving to Sydney to work in shipping, and eventually the Central Coast after he met Marjorie. They had no children, and she was his greatest joy. Her death in 2013 was devastating for him. Their home had been a haven for pets: dogs, cat, a pair of parakeets, but Bob had gradually lost interest and became almost a recluse. Organising this trip to the UK had taken courage. He had only been over once before some forty two years ago, and was sure everything would have changed - a step into the unknown.

And so the day arrived. The Arrivals Hall at Heathrow Terminal 3 was full of expectant people awaiting their long- travelled friends and family. Jill had been unsure that she would recognise her uncle, until he had sent a recent photo. They didn't have to wait long. Sure enough, there emerged a portly gentleman with the deep tan and unique facial hue left by the Australian sun. Jill approached and hugged the bewildered man.

'Uncle Bob, welcome to England.'

'G'day my dear. Good to be here.' His broad accent was unmistakable.

Dave came forward and gave him a firm handshake.

'So, you're Dave. Pleased to meet you.'

Dave grabbed Bob's old style suitcase, surprisingly light for a long distance traveller, and they moved towards the car park, somewhat lost for words on this historic family occasion. Jill broke the silence.

'So how was your trip?'

'Very good. One stop in Abu Dhabi. Slept well. I don't care for flight entertainment, I'm a simple soul.'

The pure, richly Aussie accent rolled like honey over them, as much fascinated by the way he spoke as what he said.

'Feeling tired?' asked Jill.

'Oh no, ready for anything.' Bob replied confidently.

Bob walked slowly, his big frame determining his measured gait.

'So this is Mother England. Forty two years after I last saw her. There was no internet or smartphone then,' chuckled Bob.

Jill smiled. 'Seems like another age. The world of the 1970s.'

They reached the car, settled Bob in the back seat, put his luggage in the boot and drove home. It was a warm July afternoon.

'The fields are so green.' Bob was gazing out of the window as they sped down the motorway.

The contrast between Home Counties England and the arid bush land of sunbaked New South Wales was almost total. Yet few people had the opportunity to travel halfway round the world to see the difference.

'Your houses. Like small boxes.' The spacious single storey properties of the Australian landscape contrasted again with their more compact UK counterparts.

Dave felt speechless and surprised. Never having visited Australia, he didn't appreciate anywhere could be different.

'We'll soon be home and you can rest for a few days,' said Jill. 'Any plans?'

'None, just happy to be here. I'm all yours.'

Not the reply that Dave wanted to hear.

They duly arrived home, and Bob was shown his room, while Jill prepared dinner. Dave uncorked a bottle of Chablis for the occasion, hoping it would lubricate the conversation. They sat down.

'So, all these years have passed. How is life out there, and how are you feeling about life on your own now?' Jill asked the expected open question.

Bob hesitated.

'It's not easy, that's for sure... But it's my home, where I belong.' Bob grew emotional. 'Dear Marg, I nursed her through her last illness. Died at home and in peace. I didn't touch anything in the room for months. But gradually you get the energy to move on. The reasons I'm here: first the opportunity now I'm single again, only myself to please, second you have to push yourself to do something different. Seemed a long time since I saw England, and I doubt there'll be another visit. So here I am.'

He went on.

'Don't fuss over me please. I take things slowly which is why I allowed three months, but I can amuse myself. I have a friend in Cornwall so would like to get down there sometime, but otherwise slow days are fine for me. I like to sit outside in the garden or stroll round the park. I may decide to return to Oz early, but why rush? If you enjoy something, take time over it.'

'That's fine, Uncle Bob. We can do it whichever way you want,' Jill said soothingly.

'Do you like golf?' asked Dave.

'I haven't played in years, and I'm probably a bit slow for you,' remarked Bob. 'So think I'll pass on that.'

'OK, but the offer's there.'

'Well let's toast my excellent hosts,' said Bob grabbing the initiative and the wine glass.

Everyone toasted with warm smiles. Dave was warming to their new guest. They ate the apple strudel dessert before retiring to the living room for coffee.

Jill produced some family photos, which fascinated their visitor.

'I like the one of Ted and me at the old house, when I was last here. Would love a copy of that.'

Ted was Jill's father, deceased some years ago.

'Love the family one,' chuckled Bob.

And so the evening wound to a close.

'Time to retire,' said Bob, standing up and making his way to the bedroom. 'Goodnight all.'

'Goodnight.'

Breakfast the following morning was a leisurely affair. Bob was content to sit out in the garden, admiring the flowerbeds and listening to the birds.

'July is our coldest month, but your warmest,' commented Bob. 'Look at those sparrows fighting.

We have myna birds in New South Wales, taller, with black heads.'

'I enjoy hearing the sound of the parakeets and galahs. It's different here, softer sound, more twittering and less raucous.'

Dave had never been one to appreciate birds, or study nature, but could understand that if you slowed down, you could observe more. Gardens for him meant lawns to mow.

A thrush settled briefly on the garden bench before flying off again. Bob was admiring a pair of butterflies circling each other, followed by the drone of bees passing from flower to flower.

'So much to see. You have nice geraniums, and hibiscus,' observed the visitor. 'Your roses in full bloom, so much colour.'

Dave was unsure which flowers were geraniums, but nodded in agreement.

'Shall we take a walk in the park?' asked Jill.

'Sure thing, I'll get ready.'

They were away about an hour, Bob fascinated by the trees and foliage.

'Haven't seen those in years,' he commented of oak and beech trees, 'we have so many gum trees back home that it becomes a bit monotonous, but you have several different species here.'

The afternoon was again spent in the garden, in the shade created by the house, Bob having a brief nap followed by the joy of further quiet observation Jill produced afternoon tea on a tray.

Another leisurely dinner and Bob was brimming contentment. The pace suited him nicely. No interest in going far.

And so the time passed. Slow days in bright sunshine. A few neighbours called in and enjoyed chatting to Bob. A four mile walk in nearby hills found him in his element, surrounded by the natural world, observing everything.

It didn't take much to make him happy - no need for expensive days out. Bob did do the occasional trip away but was essentially a home body enjoying the ambience of Jill and Dave's home. He did eventually get down to Cornwall, and left England after ten weeks, content with his stay, and loved by his hosts.

A NEW START

'Up a bit… no it won't go. We'll have to lift it over the banisters.'

The move was in full swing, the removals van having arrived two hours after Brian had picked up the keys to the house.

The three workmen were fitting two ropes round the wardrobe while putting a thick rubber sheet over the banister.

'Ready, heave… nearly… a bit more, that's it. I've got it. Go the other side of me and lower it.'

The antique item now stood on the landing, but still needed to go through the doorway of the back bedroom. It was too tall for that, so was once again put on its side, and, with handles unscrewed, just squeezed through the entrance with inches to spare.

'Phew… six inches wider and we would have been stuffed,' commented Bert, the self-appointed leader of the three. 'Sometimes you have to be lucky.'

He positioned the wardrobe in the corner of the room, and put the handles back on, wondering if it was going to move for another twenty years. That would be someone else's problem.

Next came the queen-size bed, also requiring base and mattress to be lifted over the landing banister, but though bulky, these were much lighter. Thereafter the chest of drawers came up the stairs, as also the smaller items, such as the chairs and two ottomans. Over the next two hours it was all done. Six heavy tea chests full of carefully wrapped china were deposited in the kitchen ready for Pat to begin the laborious process of unpacking.

Brian thanked and tipped the men. Everything accounted for. The van side roller door was duly closed, and away it went. So here they were at last in their new home.

'23 Braemar Gardens, our life starts here,' said Brian looking out at the road. A new chapter in their lives about to start.

'Yes… it hasn't really sunk in yet,' replied Pat, 'I'll believe it all in a few days.'

He put his arm round her shoulder. Finally, after months of dreaming, they had made it. It had been worth all the hard work. Endless Saturdays spent with estate agents viewing properties, debating the merits, phoning back, and widening their area of interest when it all seemed too difficult. They had lost out on an attractive semi-detached home, Pat's favourite, having had their offer initially accepted and then within hours refused. Back to square one, trying to summon up the energy to get interested again. Then they had found this house, attractively positioned in a quiet cul-de-sac. They followed their instincts, and never lost the positive feel.

Brian had yesterday borrowed the front door key and judiciously placed a bottle of champagne with a card and flowers in the bay window of the downstairs back reception room. He was hoping she would soon notice it, and sure enough within minutes a loud exclamation confirmed just that.

'Darling how nice… you did this yourself?'

They kissed and he searched hurriedly for some glasses. Finding only two unwrapped mugs, he popped the cork and poured the bottle's frothy contents into each.

'Cheers, to us and our new home.'

'To us, and many happy days ahead!'

They toasted and drank. A precious moment of satisfaction and hope. The warm July sunshine added to their optimism.

This was their new start. Recently married, they had much to look forward to.

Brian checked the meter. They had arranged a new electricity account and sure enough the power was on. Next task would be to turn on the boiler. Slowly they resumed the arduous task of unpacking, ticking off each tea chest number from their list of twenty, as also the trunk and six suitcases of carefully packed clothes.

Unsure of where to begin, Brian went to the garage and started assembling the lawn mower and positioning the two ladders, and their bikes. Then he opened boxes marked 9, 11 and 12, that comprised his tools. He unpacked nails, screws, and bolts in their carefully labelled jars, and put them on the new shelves. This would be his domain, and already he had more hook and shelf space than he had known, inviting him to expand his growing collection.

Pat meanwhile lined the cupboard shelves before carefully unpacking the kitchenware, each item carefully placed, then re-placed as her thinking changed. It was all about the best use of unfamiliar space. She checked the drawers and hooks. Enough space for now.

They had taken the advice of friends to live in the house a year before embarking on redecoration. The faded wallpaper of the reception rooms was acceptable. Ideas would come and go, improvements would suggest themselves, but that was for later. They had achieved the move from a rented two bedroom flat to a semi-detached house. One step at a time.

The afternoon moved to early evening. They stopped to order some pizza from a nearby take away, and resumed till darkness fell. Pat had put out enough bedding, and they both fell asleep from sheer fatigue. The sun had set on a memorable day. By the end of tomorrow, the unpacking would be mostly done.

'Hi, I'm Phil... Phil Jennings. Live opposite, number 26. Saw you move in yesterday.'

'Hello, nice to meet you,' said Brian, pleased to meet the neighbours. It seemed a quiet enough area, so best to keep it that way and hear the 'dos and don'ts' first hand.

'It's quiet here, really quiet. A few kids playing on the weekend. Most of the residents are families. A few elderly single people, but a good mix of ages generally. We're a friendly bunch.'

'That's good.'

'We do have a Residents' Association,' said Phil, coming to the point. 'It's a £20 yearly subscription that mainly goes toward an annual summer garden party. Unfortunately you've just missed it, but we're planning a fireworks party in November. Usually the Thompsons at number 11 oblige. We hold it in their back garden.'

'Ok, sounds great… oh by the way, which night is the rubbish collection?'

'Every fortnight on Wednesday night. The in-between week is paper and glass recycling.'

'Oh, ok.' Brian hadn't even thought about that yet.

'You know about the shortcut to the main road? Between numbers 40 and 42?'

'No. I'll check it out.'

'Ok, good I'll leave you in peace, but if you need anything, don't hesitate.'

'Thanks. Will do.'

Brian was contemplating the front lawn, an area he would know intimately well in a few months' time. It needed mowing now, but he had more important tasks to do. He noted the immaculate flowerbeds in full bloom, the work of a careful gardener. Fuchsia and petunias. Would he be able to continue that high standard? They hadn't had their own garden before.

Refocusing on current priorities, he went indoors to work out the best placement for their wall unit. It fitted nicely across the back wall of either downstairs room, with space either side. Maybe they would spend more time in the rear room, so better put it there, a question of 'what do you think?' to Pat. It had fitted perfectly against the wall in their flat, leaving Brian unsure how to use the spare space they now had on either side. One of their large vases would just fit.

Pat meanwhile was working on the living room, arranging the small items on the mantelpiece and placing their book collection in the large bookcase they had brought, now placed in the accommodating alcove.

Slowly but surely their home was taking shape. The lounge suite fitted nicely into the front room, its deep brown colour going well with the faded yellow wallpaper, with the glass coffee table positioned in front. The second reception room needed furniture, but that could wait. More pressing was the need to measure curtains to replace the threadbare ones they had inherited.

That afternoon, they made their first trip to the local supermarket, checking out the stores at the local shopping centre, and treating themselves to lunch at the carvery. Like walking on air, the feel good factor with their new environment continued, the bubble showing no sign of bursting.

'Have to invite Jim and Tanya over,' said Pat excitedly, 'bet they can't wait to see our new place. I'll email her some photos when we get back.'

'Yes, love, let's call them when we get in. Our first entertaining. I'd better buy some wine eh?' Brian was ever the organiser.

It was six months later. A cold February evening.

Brian sat motionless in the hospital corridor, too numb to feel. In the ward opposite was Pat, asleep, scarred from her recent miscarriage. The disappointment was beyond words.

Two nights ago, as Pat started to shed blood, Brian, fearing the worst, had driven her to their local hospital, St. Mary's, where immediately she was admitted, and treated for her miscarriage the following day. She had been three months pregnant.

All the hopes that the new home could lead to a new family now lay in ruins. They had married late, Brian already forty years old and Pat thirty six. Her condition, with massive fibroids, made it difficult to conceive, and they had only got this far via an IVF program. Three days before Christmas, they had been lifted by the news from the clinic that her eggs had fertilised and she was confirmed pregnant. Their year of happiness, 2015, with the house move and the promise of parenthood, had now given way to a disappointing 2016. Things were falling apart. Brian felt sorrier for Pat than for himself. He could only look on.

The realisation that this might be their only chance, given Pat's condition, now hit home. For others there would be another chance to come. For them, this was it. Further attempts were futile.

They could consider adoption, but it was highly competitive and controlled. Their names were on no one's waiting list. Children the world over needed a home, but getting them into the UK was another matter. The alternative was childlessness, which many couples might not mind, but Brian and Pat had cherished the idea of having a family. She had already been buying baby clothes in the belief that faith itself would produce a baby. She doted on her two young nephews, forever inviting them over for sleepovers, but you always had to say goodbye until next time. You really wanted your own children.

But these were all thoughts for later. The important concern was to get Pat home and rested. Miscarriage had mental effects too. You had to keep busy to avoid dwelling on the loss. Brian was already planning a fortnight's holiday abroad for them both. Beyond that he wanted to help Pat set up a shop in their local arcade, selling second-hand books and videos. They had often talked about it. There was nothing like this available locally, which Brian attributed to the growth of the worldwide web and downloaded movies, but there was always a market for older technology. E-books had not yet replaced books. Success came with diversification to the limit of the retail licence: books, CDs, DVDs, artwork. Something for everyone.

Two days later, Pat was discharged and Brian drove her home. She rested in bed while he sat beside her.

'Not much to say really,' she murmured.

'It's OK. You'll be all right, and can rest well over the next few weeks.' Brian tried to encourage her, trying also to encourage himself, though unsuccessfully.

'Glad that I've got you darling. You look after me so well,' she said.

'You've been through a lot. It's mental as much as physical, and none of it pleasant. Just take it slowly.' He held out his hand for her to touch.

'OK dear, I will. I'll try and get some sleep now.' She sounded tired.

'All right, I'll wake you with some dinner a bit later.'

There really wasn't much conversation to have. They both knew that there was little chance now for them to have their own children. However you sweeten the pill, it was the same message, left unsaid, in their minds. People talk of moving on, but sometimes it is so so hard. Everything may happen for a reason but it's sometimes baffling to understand what that is.

Yet slowly but surely, the healing process started. The sense of loss hung around them like a heavyweight, but it wasn't the end. Life and hope continued, faith in a better tomorrow. They just had to believe; the path was often tortuous.

DISPOSSESSED

Carl is a wonderful son. The home videos of ten years ago show a bubbly toddler tearing open his birthday presents, wearing cream and chocolate all over his smiling face, riding his tricycle. Happy with life, happy with his family, beaming love to all.

He runs out into the garden, finding his digger and rides it down the path to the sandpit, where he digs furiously with his spade, as if buried treasure existed underneath. Furious energy and purpose, that's Carl, gurgling joyfully as he digs. Kevin smiled, seeing something of himself in his son. Was I really like that? Being an only child, there was always the danger of Carl being spoilt - doting grandparents on both sides of the family lavishing birthday gifts on him. But he mixed well with other children, good in the group, dutifully waiting his turn on the playground slide.

There was Carl's first bike with the training wheels. Taking him round the pavements of their cul-de-sac, lap after lap. 'Come on Dad, more, more.' Kevin found himself increasingly drawn into a second childhood. Playing football, cycling, building Lego, reading books, they had so much time together, so much bonding, father and son. Putting Carl to bed after a full day, seeing him slip into sleep, smiling to himself with contentment. All so wonderful.

And so came nursery and then school at age four and a half. Carl loved it: new friends, new experiences - happiness on a stick.

Sometimes though we have to capture that happiness on camera because of its transience - here today, gone tomorrow. The moments of greatest joy sit alongside those of greatest pain. The joyful, excited child of a minute ago now tripping over and bawling his eyes out.

Kevin flicked through the photo album: Carl at the playground, Carl at the caravan park, Carl on the beach - all innocently taken, as if a lifetime ago. The beauty of yesterday. A child lives in a loving home with a bright future ahead of him - a family portrait, Wendy holding Carl. Yes, Wendy…

Times change, people change. You never know what will happen next in life. Wendy, whom he had adored, who had made such a happy home, and used to welcome him home each evening with news of what Carl had done at school that day. Wendy, who organised picnic baskets to take on country walks, and welcomed Carl's friends to the house, with a beautiful smile for everyone. Wendy, who had no hint of anything disagreeable in her manner. Fun-loving Wendy, organising the Halloween party, lighting the candles in the pumpkins, bringing out the jacket potatoes. Wendy, who farewelled each child with a homemade goodie bag, full of chat as she cleared up afterwards.

Yes, this was the same Wendy who now grew distant and dogmatic, thinking the worst, and isolating herself from family life. Why you may ask? What switch had been flicked? For Kevin the same question resonated with almost hourly frequency. What had he done or not done? What should he know, to be able to help? Was it psychiatric? And what impact did it have on Carl? Many nights of reflection, of looking for information on the laptop, had failed to answer these questions.

Imponderable questions have no easy answers. What is, is. Kevin had thought that depression was the problem. Wendy had no paid job, though she was well immersed in the school community with coffee mornings, and volunteering two days a week at a local charity shop. She viewed herself as a 'people person', so no shortage of friends or company. Was it lack of fulfilment? The need for change but no change possible? If so, why not voice it, discuss a new role, see how it can work in the family life? But there was no discussion, no clue as to what was working in her mind, just a feeling that she was retreating into herself.

The long look into the mirror leads to the analysis of self. Dark forces take over if you let them, working like seeds inside the mind before sprouting like weeds, taking over the good soil if you don't act. So it seemed with Wendy. Slowly, gradually, she became someone else, but never discussed a thing, as if her mind now belonged to an alien, completely taken over. She started sleeping alone, keeping odd hours, her face reflecting anxiety, her conversation defensive.

Kevin tried talking to her but got cut off each time, encouraging her to see a doctor. He suggested time away, but she gave every impression of wanting to avoid him. She was still good with Carl, but tried to be too possessive of him, eroding the quality of Kevin's time with his son.

And then, suddenly, she was demanding a split, talking about taking Carl and going to live with her mother. Kevin dismissed it at first, but she kept repeating it until finally it happened, as if she was uncaring of the consequences. Kevin came home one day and they were gone - no note, no furniture removed, but importantly Carl, his lovely boy, gone. He was eight, loving school and his friends, enthusiastic about everything. Once she resumed communication, there was a terrific argument over schooling, but eventually she enrolled him in a primary school in Hull close to her new home. Kevin had been left to take in a lodger for some months, before putting the house up for sale and moving to a two-bedroom flat. But there was no Carl to build models or play computer games with, just an empty home to return to after work, a presence sorely missed.

What you once had, you no longer have. It's taken from you, to leave you with fading memories. Dispossessed of his lovely son, his pride and joy, Kevin felt numb. A boy you could lift and shake, whose giggles filled the silence, who delighted in his Dad, was gone. There was now just silence and emptiness. Instead, Carl was a six-hour drive away, to be visited by monthly appointment, and taken away somewhere, but not to a home where he could relax with his dad. A rented motel room was the best they could manage, overnight, before Carl had to be returned and Kevin contemplated the long, lonely drive home, aggrieved at being put through all this.

The once bubbly boy was now subdued. A meek 'Hi Dad,' and a weak smile, as if uncertain that he wanted to come out. He would soon revert to a happier manner once the day's plan was revealed; a cinema visit to see the latest cartoon movie or a trip to an adventure playground. But it was painful to be restricted to a fixed time, as if the psychology of the midday Sunday return deadline spoiled their time together.

Carl and Dad. Dad and Carl. The warmth was still there, but they were no longer the inseparables. However, the physical picking up or tickling his son still brought out the giggles. The excitement of being together, going to a theme park or eating at a favourite restaurant, was still there; so was the chance to buy the merchandise of the latest movie, the tee shirt and the toy. Experiences were still shared together, from watching TV programs, to cycling round a park, to assembling the latest spaceship kit. The bond was more tenuous but yet unbreakable. Longer distance apart and shorter time together were unable to sever the ties of fatherhood.

'Dad, school isn't fun.'

It seemed hard for him to make friends up here. Never a problem when they lived in Hertfordshire, but a real issue here in Hull. Carl's first birthday since coming here was due in a few weeks, and Kevin worried that it wouldn't be a happy one.

'I want the big kit, Spaceship Galatica, for my birthday.'

'OK mate, I'll get it, and bring it up next visit.'

But the logistics of sitting in a motel room, painstakingly assembling the structure incompletely, before having to take it all home, were evident to Kevin. He no longer had a home with his son.

More than anything he was angry with Wendy for the effect all this had had on Carl - the anger of bitter disappointment but not hatred. Once you hated, you had lost, and despite having the dice loaded against him, Kevin was still hanging in there. Their once bright, lovely boy was now confused, quiet, uncertain why his Dad wasn't at home but came to visit instead. He was also adapting to life in a different part of the country, with different accents and local words he didn't understand. If she had to do this, why not wait till the boy was older, maybe eleven years old and changing schools?

Two or three years were significant for Carl. He was too young to handle all this now. But now Wendy was talking about divorce as if it was the next step in a plan. She never even came to the front door, but instead let Carl let himself out - convenience covering embarrassment.

Life goes on and so did Kevin's. Every so often, he allowed himself to reflect on the huge burden of time and expense involved in seeing his beloved boy, and the limitations placed whenever that occurred. In winter, especially, it was inhospitable outdoors, and the only option was to watch TV in the motel room, or play whatever games Carl brought in his rucksack. There was no option to move around to another room or prepare a snack. They made the best of it. Something was better than nothing, the refusal of the human spirit to allow brokenness to have the last word. But it took effort and sacrifice to get there. Sometimes Kevin would stay overnight before travelling back, hating every minute of being there without his son, scraping ice off the windscreen for his 6 am departure.

September 14th - Carl's ninth birthday. His party was scheduled for the Saturday 12th, so Kevin decided to come up the following weekend. It was the first time he had missed being with Carl on the actual day.

Buying the Spaceship Galatica kit was no problem, its £89 price tag indicating it was bigger and better than any previous model. Sadness came in the knowledge that father and son would be unable to complete assembling this structure together. The twenty-four hour window of the visit was insufficient to do much more than check out the parts, read the instructions, and make a start. The rest Carl would have to do himself at home, alone and in isolation, unless he waited a month and brought all the pieces back to the motel room, an unlikely option.

The gift was meticulously wrapped in Carl's favourite black and white striped paper. No football team allegiance here, but just the curiosity of seeing two opposite colours beside each other, the extremes of life. Then the card, carefully chosen and signed, was stuck to the front of the spaceship. A colourful carrier bag completed the set, all ready to be delivered.

Kevin had a good run up the motorway, reaching the house in just under five hours.

'Hi Dad, did you get it?'

'Sure did.'

When they arrived at the motel, no sooner was the gift presented, than the paper was quickly torn apart in true Carl style.

'Wow, Dad that's great. Let's start it.'

'How was your party?'

'I only had two friends over to the house. We played 'Road Rally', and had a cake. It was ok.'

Kevin said nothing. He remembered Carl's eighth birthday, with twelve children in the garden, a treasure hunt, and a big cake with lots of candles. All now a distant memory.

'I brought a small cake for you,' said Kevin, producing it from the bag. They opened a bottle of lemonade to go with it, a private celebration.

'Thanks Dad, nice.'

'To you and number nine.'

Kevin poured it into plastic cups and they toasted.

Now it was time to open the big box and take out the numerous plastic bags that made up the Galatica kit, look into each and identify where to start.

Two trays, remembered by Kevin, helped hold the many tiny pieces spilling out of the bags. Carl took charge, working out what fitted to what, and moving quickly on, a study in concentration.

He started one section, absorbed for a full hour fitting parts to make a sub-assembly, and then combined several of them into a finished assembly, in turn to fit into something bigger.

'Finished the landing craft, let's start the base.'

It was nice for Kevin to play the minor role, watch his son's quick thinking. The room table was slowly filling with the assembled sections, that later would fit together into the whole spaceship.

Time had gone so fast that Kevin had almost forgotten to order food. They went down to the diner for a break, ordering chicken and chips, Carl's favourite, followed by a knickerbocker glory to mark the special occasion. Nine years old. Next year would be double figures, 10, a milestone birthday, Carl moving away from childhood. Kevin asked one of the diners to take a photo of them both, to retain the memory, so quickly passing, but now marked for ever.

'Thanks Dad that was so yummy.'

Back up the room they watched TV for a while, a family show with crazy games that made them both laugh. A chance to forget the restrictions of their meeting and relax. Soon it would be bedtime for Carl, and Kevin didn't linger long after. It had been a happy day.

Sunday morning came with its sobering predictability, and while Carl wasn't due back to Wendy's mother's house till noon, the looming deadline cast its shadow over their time together.

After a leisurely brunch, they checked out and drove to a large park with a playground, spending their last hour together there.

The part-finished spaceship had been carefully wrapped, and each plastic bag put into a carrier bag brought for the purpose. The logistics of ensuring the spaceship parts were all brought home, and none were missing, was an operation in itself.

Then came the customary farewell.

'Bye Dad. Thanks, enjoyed it.'

Kevin hugged him.

'Bye son, see you soon.'

The front door was quickly shut and that was that. The end of this special visit, nothing to contemplate now except the long journey home. After a few moments Kevin started the car and moved off, his mind reflecting on many things. His son had been his for a short while but now no longer. What had been so natural and happy a few years ago, was now complicated by a barrier of dispossession, as Carl, not through choice, was moving into a place Kevin couldn't reach.

Six hours later, he was home to his apartment. It was early evening, but he went straight to bed, wanting to close the chapter on a special weekend.

But with a feeling of triumph in his big heart.

THE MASTER

'And that's checkmate, I think… yes mate.' Frank moved his knight beside his bishop to remove any chance of the king's escape.

He looked up and smiled at his opponent. It had been a long game, over two hours, between two evenly matched players, but as so often, a break in concentration, with a resulting mistake, had decided the contest. Eric nodded and smiled graciously, beaten again by the one man he couldn't better. The titanic duel of the chess club's elite left him yet again in second place.

For Frank, the purist, it was almost more important not to lose than to win. His disciplined approach had been tested over the years and he could only remember three defeats in the last ten years. The lessons from each had been well learnt, the chinks in his armour plugged, and his watchfulness redoubled.

He prided himself on his uniquely cautious approach, based on intense concentration, and never put off by the mannerisms of opponents. Each move, even at the start, was carefully weighed before placement, his fingers holding the piece in place before slowly releasing it and then pressing the timer. Rarely would he be surprised. The key was to become your opponent and imagine their best moves, wondering why, sometimes, they didn't make them.

He was also an addict for the newspaper chess puzzles, working out how to force checkmate in four moves from a particular setting, assuming the mindset of the author.

Chess is the pictorial image of what is going on in the human mind. As we think, so we play. It can be a quick win or excruciatingly slow, as strategies to conquer are frustrated. Perhaps that was the ultimate appeal of chess, that no two games over the centuries are ever the same. Thought pattern A meets thought pattern B, and we all think differently. Get the knight out early? Create a diagonal line of pawns? Clear a path for the bishops? Instinct often overrides reason.

The attraction for Frank was the symmetry - pieces arranged in order, king's bishop, knight and castle matching their queen counterparts. It was everything that life wasn't: tidy, complete, conforming to rules, each player with the same strength, the true level playing field. Life, by contrast, pitted players of unequal strength against each other, some with the full set of pieces, others with bishops and knights missing, or with just a king and a few pawns, and the remaining pieces never there. Employer versus employee, landlord against tenant, superpower against small nation. Chess was fair, life wasn't and didn't pretend to be. It was what it was.

But the contrast was not as marked as might be thought. There was benefit in approaching life with some caution, mindful of the moves that other players planned, and careful to avoid exposing oneself to danger. It was in reality a three dimensional game, with multiple opponents or parties, perhaps not always identified as having opposed interests. Strategy and tactics were required. Projects needed an approach and a set of moves to reach a goal, be that applying for further education or constructing an urban bypass. Along the way were obstacles requiring workarounds or removal, and the outcome could not be easily predicted. And then there was the sense of deep frustration when you have three or four moves stymied by your opponent, so typical of life. Sometimes you feel locked in, unable to progress.

Chess was also a game with ancient and royal origins. Pawns were like infantry, slowly marching forward in formation, nuisance value to the opponent's major pieces. Knights really would have been mounted on horseback in bygone days, twisting and turning in the heat of battle. Bishops had their long diagonal sweeps, and the impersonal, but equally powerful castles ruled the outer edge. The queen, with her range of moves contrasted with the one square limping of the king, a form of role reversal for the male-dominated Persian civilisations from which this game originated. The origin of the moves was lost in the mists of time.

One of the beauties of chess was its sets, so lovingly created - beautifully sculptured, almost personalised figures: the king with a face, crown, and robes, bishops with mitres and castles (rooks) with thick turrets. They were works of art in themselves. Placing pieces at the start, and putting them away in position in the box afterwards, enhanced one's respect for the sacred nature of the game. Frank had a two hundred year old ivory set that he still played with on a large board, having no sympathy with the view that older sets were only there for show and not for use. The layout was that of a battle re-enactment, with the foot soldier pawns giving way to higher, intricately carved major pieces. The queen was a regal woman, just as the crowned king looked a distinguished man, and the horse-head knights were replaced by armoured figures. Black gave way to red for colour, while the grid-like set box allowed taken pieces to be appropriately placed. Examination of them gave clues as to the state of the game.

Frank played several games a week, usually of an evening, at home with his elder son, or at the

Wednesday night meeting of the Hadleigh Chess Club in the local parish hall. There were around twelve regulars, mainly retired men, sitting in six paired bubbles of concentrated silence. The timers allowed five minutes per go, and games could often run for two hours, incomplete by the close. Piece positions were carefully noted, ready for the resumption, with different mindsets in a week's time. Occasionally this was repeated, so that games of five or six hours reached their inexorable conclusion. The junior section of the club encouraged starters or students from school chess clubs who needed to sharpen their skills, while games of suicide chess at the end of the evening provided some light relief over brewed coffee and cake.

As for competitions, well there were plenty of those too, Hadleigh versus local villages, led by team captain, Frank, with five of the better players making up the team. Contests had been random before a local league was formed a few years ago, once a month on a Thursday. Cumulative points for wins, and bonus points for duration went towards the final placings, Hadleigh invariably coming in the top two. Chess was a game of skill, not of luck, and hence the position reflected the strength of the club, with each victory merited.

And so it was that the Grand Master Tournament developed, a competition to find the finest chess player in Wessex. The county had advertised for players in local papers and online, shortlisting thirty two nominees who were tasked with playing off through preliminary rounds to quarterfinals, semis and a final. The winner would be duly crowned Grand Master.

Frank was not slow to put himself forward, and duly progressed to the quarterfinals without difficulty. Here he came up against a Czech opponent, Mr. Stanislaw, likewise noted for his attention to detail. It was perhaps an unfortunate pairing at this stage, given that the match would have been a worthy final. The game had passed the two-hour mark before Frank made a key strike, trapping his opponent's bishop and then putting his king in check in a series of moves to maintain the offensive. Mr. Stanislaw stabilised the situation, and pushed Frank's knight and rook back. But Frank's superiority of pieces eventually told, and he was able to clean up some pawns allowing his queen free rein. Soon after, he forced checkmate, watched by a number of observers who had completed their own games already. The long, arduous battle had been decided; by far the closest and longest match of the contest to date.

It was another few days before the semi-final took place, with Frank paired against Bob Elliot of Bathampton, likewise a leader in his area. Bob had worked his pawn strategy well, restricting Frank's moves such that the game looked to be deadlocked at one stage. It was the familiar situation of an inability to move; suppressed energy looking for an outlet. Knights were unable to find a safe square while bishops were blocked from getting out. Eventually, a few risks broke up the board, and Bob grabbed the initiative, taking Frank's rook and forcing two successive checks. But Frank was a survivor, and gradually came back into the match, with a co-ordinated attack from his remaining rook and two bishops. Thereafter, pieces were swapped, and finally Frank brought his queen into play and trapped Bob's knight, eventually forcing mate. Another respected opponent smiled, commented and shook hands. Frank had now progressed to the final, to be held with audience and overhead screen next Sunday afternoon in a large church hall in Westport. Interest had swelled and around a hundred spectators were expected.

For a mental sport, chess ranks high, demanding skill and concentration. 'Give the best and get the best. Think laterally, use the power of all the pieces at your disposal. Understand economy of moves, achieving in three what could take five. Remember the game is about checkmating the opponent's king, not taking as many of his/her pieces as possible. Sometimes that helps, sometimes it wastes time. An opponent will always interrupt your game plan so execute it quickly. Don't allow your opponent to dictate the game.'

These were all the tips Frank gave the others, and now himself had to reaffirm. Sunday's match didn't rank at the same level as a team sport cup final, but nevertheless required preparation, and generated some excitement. Two different coloured shirts had been made, yellow for Frank, representing Hadleigh, and red for Richard Blake of Tattersham, another key player widely respected around the county. The inaugural prize, a silver trophy, had been made especially for the occasion. There was just enough flair to enliven the occasion without removing its innate dignity.

And so the day arrived.

'Ready for it? You look remarkably calm,' commented, Helen, Frank's wife.

'It's just another game. Keep to the basics,' he replied, giving nothing away. Other than a good night's sleep and an hour's walk to clear the mind, he had done nothing else. It was hard to study your opponent till you played him.

They drove down to Westport and parked the car, before walking through the main door of the building with its 'Wessex Chess Grand Master 2016' banner. The hall was filling, an umpire had been appointed, and soon the players were seated.

'Mr. Frank Bates of the Hadleigh club will be playing Mr. Richard Blake from the Tattersham club. The winner will be the Wessex Chess Grand Master,' the smartly dressed umpire announced.

A coin was tossed, and Frank, losing the toss, took black.

'Mr. Blake takes white and will start. Please observe silence during the moves, with any applause at the end of each move.'

Richard got his king's knight out first in a quick safe move, while Frank took his time to advance his pawns. The next few exchanges involved Richard moving bishops out, while Frank created space in front of his main pieces by advancing his pawns in formation, suffocating the white pieces - two different approaches. The results on the overhead projector were closely studied by the audience, despite the fact that chess was not seen as a spectator sport.

The intensity required some light relief, but each contestant was reluctant to break the silence in case he was thought to be taking an advantage. Time out was offered every half hour - a chance to get up from the table and breathe fresh air, while being carefully kept away from the audience. Frank was deep in thought, a number of options circulating through his mind. He needed to get his pieces out beyond his line of pawns.

The match resumed. Frank started to move his main pieces forward, then castled to give his rook a direct line of attack on the white King. Richard took two of his pawns in the process of breaking out, his bishops pinning the black queen.

Thrust and counterthrust, but all was proceeding slowly, like black clouds before a storm. Something had to give.

It is possible in chess to play minor moves forwards and backwards to suffocate the match, and such appeared the situation here. The game was waiting for a mistake and uncharacteristically it was Frank who made it, as he would afterwards reflect. He lost his bishop to Richard's knight, and thus lost his hold on the white queen. It was avoidable. His king was twice in check, and he was losing control. The hushed audience looked surprised.

The break came, and Frank took stock. He had a knight, bishop, two rooks and a queen left, all in promising positions. Richard had only lost a rook. His pieces were more dispersed than Frank's, not so supportive of each other. The resumption saw Frank take two pawns, and push his knight very close to the white king. Next he forced check with his bishop. He was on the way back. Richard had to defend fast and lost a rook in a piece swap with Frank's knight. But Frank was pushing his pawns right up, and sure enough one of them went the whole way to the end to claim a second queen. It was now just a matter of time. The two queen and bishop combination took control and tied Richard down. Three moves later the match was over, Richard graciously conceding. Handshakes all round.

'And the first Grand Master of Wessex is Mr. Frank Bates of Hadleigh,' announced the umpire.

The trophy was handed to him by the town mayor.

The Hadleigh applause broke out. The contest had lasted two and a half hours, patiently followed by the assembled throng. Frank glowed, his face for once reflecting his inner emotions. It had been tough there for a while. Thank goodness he had held onto his pawns. The smallest piece becoming, as queen, the largest.

All done, or was it? For Frank it was just another game. Tomorrow was his next. The master never pauses.

THE PURCHASE

It was that time again. A time that recurs every three to four years for some, and less frequently for others. A realisation, working its way slowly from the subconscious to the conscious, that a change would be good.

Tom's 2008 Nissan Qashqai, with 150,000 miles on the clock and some significant maintenance expense looming, was due an upgrade. Time to check out the dealers, and the online offerings. See how much he could get for a Trade In. The pleasant anticipation of something new tempered with the need to be careful, to do due diligence. That was the key to success.

His teaching commitments didn't allow any progress for a few weeks, and the issue lay waiting, biding its time. Being a single man in his early twenties, time was on Tom's side. No one else to consider here.

Whoever came closely into his life in the next few years could tolerate his taste, at least initially. No aging parents to run around, or children requiring a people carrier. No in-depth justification to make to nearest and dearest. Those days were ahead of him. All he needed was plenty of luggage space, leg room, good front and rear speakers for entertainment, and quick acceleration. A car to attract envy perhaps, but there was nothing cynical about Tom, no hidden agenda. Cars were functional, and no amount of smart image marketing would change his thinking.

It was on the way back from a school Saturday rugby fixture that Tom called in at Stewart Nissan, the big dealership close to home. A preliminary 'look and see' to check what was out there, get the brain cells moving, grab a brochure and so on. Sitting at a desk in front of a friendly salesman, discussion soon narrowed Tom's choices to suit his budget. The rep showed him round some of the recent models, including the recently introduced Procentra, named in Spanish, as if to create an aura of mystique around a less exotic looking five door hatchback.

And there it was, the second car viewed, a deep dark blue coloured model, gleaming in the late afternoon sun.

'You'll like this one sir,' said the rep knowingly.

You bet, this was it. Someone had looked after this car lovingly, indeed with just over 10,000 miles on the clock, had seldom used it, as if waiting to hand it on. Tom walked round it, almost scared to touch, then opened a door and eased himself into its soft cushioned passenger seat. Wow, comfortable! It felt good, plenty of legroom. He looked ahead at the bright clean dashboard, opened the glove box. The salesman, Rod, was busily demonstrating some features. Hmmm.... nice car. This was worth a test drive.

Rod readily commented on interest already received in the car, as if taking it off the forecourt for a twenty minute drive would somehow deprive him of yet more prospective customers. Unfazed, Tom took the wheel over from him and drove it round the block, hoping in some muddled way that a problem might surface, thus making it easier to reject the car, and let him revisit a prospective purchase at his leisure. But no, the engine purred as he swiftly moved up the gears to a smooth fifth. It was begging to be taken for a motorway spin. This was his car, he felt sure. He had the feeling in his bones.

Now came the inner battle between him and himself, the two inseparables. Often living in harmony, but sometimes as now, in conflict. The rational versus the emotional, head against heart, surfacing when a major expense was contemplated. The impulsive, feel good self reacting to the disciplined, logical inner man. The fun-loving evening drinker clashing with the sobriety of the morning-after hangover. The yin and the yang of personality, though Tom doubted that between them they made a perfect whole. Just two sides of his multiple-dimensional character, he supposed, being unsure what the other sides showed.

So, whether to buy or not? It certainly wasn't the first car he had bought. Experience told him to do his research online, then visit the dealers, particularly to see their valuation of the Qashqai, but here he was, falling for the first model he had seen, before even turning on the iPad. Plush upholstery, feeling of space, a state of the art dashboard, satnav, copious boot space, there was much to savour. A 2014 model, only eighteen months old, low mileage, deep marine blue colour, immaculate interior, shiny alloy wheels, and a turbo-powered engine which you could certainly feel. Hmmmm, what not to like. Well the price tag of course, £14,999. Some flexibility on that perhaps but the real question was how much they would give him for the Qashqai. They'd rather throw in a free service and take-away meal vouchers than offer much back. Price was everything. Well it was now late Saturday afternoon, and he would have two nights to sleep on it, doubtless waking up tomorrow wondering why on earth he had ever considered it. A sobering look at the private sales would surely jolt him into realising that the same year model was available for £2000 less, the difference paying for slick dealer presentation.

But then, instinctively, it felt so right. He could see himself driving it. Nothing awkward on the drive; it handled really well. You could see a hundred more cars and not feel the same. Instinct was a pretty reliable friend. The only person he had to impress was himself, no wife or girlfriend. Taste not status won the mental fight, and he had been here before. Compromise on that and you run into problems. You're not buying the car for someone else.

He drove home to his riverside apartment deep in thought. Time to check the adverts, and see what else was out there, to experience the reality check of the public marketplace. At first glance there were few Procentras available. It was a newer, popular model that people preferred to keep rather than sell. But closer examination found two for sale, and Tom quickly made the appointments. That done, he could prepare for his evening engagement, dinner with two old school friends. That itself could provide a few leads and pointers.

The three of them gathered at the Kings Arms in Rippleswell - Andy, fresh from a business trip to Miami, Rob, studying for a Masters degree, and Tom himself. Three pints of best bitter ordered and the menu passed round. They retired to a corner table, deep in conversation, catching up with the news.

Andy had much to say about his first visit to USA, smitten with Florida's climate, lifestyle and breakfast bars. Rob was quieter, as if studying Local History was dull by comparison, but talked passionately about a local archaeological project that had unearthed an Iron Age settlement. Pieces of pottery and some stone tools had been discovered. Tom, in turn, gave his latest impressions of teaching, now in his second year as Physics master at a local private school. Only towards the end did he raise the topic of the new car.

'Took a test drive in a Procentra this afternoon. Smooth as anything you could hope for.'

'Really. Why don't you look for a sports car, change your image?' asked Andy.

Tom laughed. 'No, I'm more functional. As long as the golf clubs fit in the boot, I'm happy.'

'The Centaur is supposed to be good. Getting the press at the moment.'

'Oh OK, I'll check it out.' Tom wasn't aware of it, and made a mental note.

'If it was me, I'd be looking at that first,' continued Andy, 'a friend at work has one. Really cool.'

'Don't go for the Santora. Been hearing some bad stories,' added Rob, 'Cheap and nasty. You get what you pay for.'

'Anyway, cheers. Good luck with it.'

They raised their glasses, and toasted Tom's venture, before the conversation moved on to sport, and Tom's efforts with the first XV rugby, whose three quarters lacked the pace to threaten most oppositions.

Dinner soon arrived, and Rob regaled them with his new-found love of rowing. They chatted on, not noticing the time, and soon concluded an enjoyable evening.

Tom rose late on Sunday morning, having lain in bed contemplating his next move with the car. He felt somewhat rushed by events, but knew that sooner or later he needed to do his homework, and there was no time like the present. Having searched through the range of makes and models of interest, including the Centaur, he was still positive on the Procentra. Good reviews in the motoring press too.

'Economical on fuel, with impressively quick acceleration,' was the verdict.

Thus encouraged, he drove over to see the lady advertising a burgundy 2012 model. Yes it presented well, drove well, but had some bumper scratches, bypassed in the 'good condition' description of the ad. He wasn't keen on the colour, so passed with politeness before driving to his second, and more hopeful, meeting with a Mr. Gibson. This was for a black two year old model, apparently being sold as part of a divorce settlement. The seller seemed down on his luck, and the price was competitive in the hope of a quick sale. Tempting… It handled well on the road, though with high mileage for its age, and some internal signs of wear. Tom didn't commit but said he would get back to the man the following day.

All his instincts still pointed towards the blue Procentra he had seen yesterday at Stewart's. His heart lay there, while his head told him to go with the black model offered at £13,500, maybe costing £13,000 at a push. You love the one and like the other. Moreover, this was a five year investment, so the extra £1,500, that the showroom model cost, would soon be forgotten, and once he negotiated, this might be a difference of a little over £1,000. Something to sleep on, and reflect over during the school Monday, as it would be late afternoon by the time he could get back to the dealer. There again, it might have gone already, leaving him with the black one, or perhaps a decision to defer. There was, after all, no urgency.

As so often happens when sleeping on a decision, sleep didn't bring clarity. Tom woke in the same quandary as yesterday. The continuity of thinking had been broken by sleep, but had resumed at the same place. This wasn't a 'phone a friend' option, only he could resolve it. Time to ponder wasn't plentiful as he was teaching the first two periods, and had to prepare for them. Hard bargaining would have to wait, not just once the school day was done, but also once his head was clear of school, and he could focus on the enormity of the purchase.

It was a frustrating Monday. Driving rain slowed his journey to school, and his class 3 pupils, first up, were particularly unresponsive. Someone should abolish weekends he had been thinking, as there appeared to be a collective brain clearance. Then half of his fifth year didn't turn up due to a clashing commitment he hadn't been told about. He was eventually informed with apology. The afternoon got somewhat easier, and with a free period at the end of the day, he arrived home early, in no mood to be buying a car. Maybe fate was telling him something.

He made some coffee and sat down in the armchair. It was 4.30pm. If hearts ruled the night, heads ruled the day, and he decide first to negotiate with Mr. Gibson, and see how far he would drop price.

'Hello, it's Tom Richardson. I called over yesterday to see the car. Is it still for sale?'

'Yes, hi, I remember you. Yes still here, but I've got someone interested coming in half an hour.'

They always said that.

'Would you be prepared to take £13,000 for it?'

Silence.

'No. Can't drop that much. This divorce is costing me a fortune.'

'Oh OK. I really can't do much more. £13,200 my last offer.'

'Let me think about it. Have to consult the ex, as it was her car. Will call you back.'

Likely story… He's just trying to defend himself, thought Tom. But it was a noticeable shift in mood. Yesterday the man had seemed to want a quick sale. Maybe he had also been thinking or maybe he really did have others interested. It didn't sound promising, and certainly Tom was not expecting the return call.

So, this was getting easier. Time to go with the heart. Mentally Tom had thought that if the difference in price between black and blue could be brought within £1000, he would go with his heart. But was it still for sale? How many others had also been mulling it over, and got back to Stewart's more quickly? And noticeably Rod, the rep, had not followed him up. Be prepared for disappointment.

'Hi Rod? It's Tom Richardson. Saw the blue Procentra on Saturday. We did a test drive.'

'Hi Tom, yes I remember well. Was going to call you. How are you doing?'

When was there ever a car salesman not about to pick up the phone?

'Good thanks. Is the car still available?'

'Yes, just. But it'll be gone by this time tomorrow for sure. You need to be quick.'

'OK, coming over. You'll still be there a while?'

'Close at 5.30pm but we're usually around till 6pm. Will be expecting you.'

'OK, see you in ten minutes.'

Promising. It was still there, still his for the taking. So far so good. He grabbed his car keys and set off.

Upon arrival, a closer look at the car did not disappoint in any way. Negotiations were soon into high gear. As expected, Rod, the salesman, was negative on the Quashqai, offering initially £2999, with feigned generosity as if he was giving away free tickets for a cruise. Through sheer persistence Tom had managed to raise that to £3999 and also get a £200 price drop on the Procentra. A free service and a full tank of petrol were thrown in, and the hour-long session was done. Tom was happy enough. Effectively a £10,000 hit after exchange, which he had always factored. Once a Cover Note had been arranged, he was driving it home. He glanced at the time, 6.45pm. It had been exhausting. All the drama saved till the end of the day. At least, he wasn't going to die wondering.

He sat in the car, scanning the registration details and an immaculately kept service log. The car handbook could be read later. He put a CD in the drive and turned on the radio, then the satnav. All fine. Seat and mirror adjusted to give perfect comfort. Remote locking and immobiliser checked. So, he was ready for the first journey to school tomorrow morning. He smiled inwardly imagining the likely comments.

The week had passed, and Tom was basking in the glow of a man who had made the right decision. Positive feedback, even envy from colleagues and friends. He had taken a few of them for a drive, and enjoyed the favourable reaction. The 'let me know when you want to sell it' kind. Full insurance cover at an economical price had been no issue, given his 60% max no claims bonus on the Qashqai. In a few weeks he planned to give it a good run to his cousin's at Nottingham, cruising on the motorway in fifth gear.

It was mid-Saturday morning, and there was the usual scrum at the 'pay and display' town car park. Tom had parked on the end of a row, while getting his weekly groceries at the supermarket, and checking the price of suits at the tailors. Tomorrow a round of golf was planned with his usual opponents at his local White Oak club.

His shopping took an hour, and laden with plastic bags he returned to the car. On rounding the corner into the car park, he dropped them in disbelief.

'No, no it can't be true.' He felt like screaming.

He stared at the front passenger door of the car, now marked half way along with a noticeable dent and scraping of white paint. Evidently, a car reversing from the spaces along the end wall had come back too far and caught the Procentra, the driver not hanging around to do the right thing and acknowledge it. Tom's new car already damaged after only five days.

He moved forward to examine the door in more detail. The tarnishing was more than the surface damage he saw. It was a wound to confidence, the bursting of the feel good bubble. The feeling of resignation, that something in life always drags you down, enveloped him; falling down the snake after climbing the long ladder in a bid to be one of life's winners. Tom was numb and speechless.

What do they say? Keep calm and carry on.

JOB SEARCH

'Project Manager required by dynamic retailing group for Pan European e-business rollout. Twelve month contract, extendable. Must have proven methodology such as SMAP5 or LITEX. Submit a CV via our portal www.zancareers.com or phone Peter Fleming on 0207 618 3555 for more details.'

Trish swallowed a mouthful of toast, as she scanned her job alerts on the iPad. Interesting, this had just come in, and was worth a phone call to check out the details. London-based, but it doubtless involved travelling around. Extendable probably meant it would run for at least two years. They'd never get the work done in less time. The rate sounded good, offered in a range, but acceptable low or high end. She was straight off a three year project for a coffee wholesaler that had used SMAP5, so that would be no problem. Trish felt herself to be in pole position.

This was one she could see herself doing. CV up to date, references at the ready. Bring it on.

She was just back from a three week mid-winter break in the Greek Islands with her husband, Ken. A chance to recharge the batteries after the high pressure of Fowler's Coffee. There, a two year, very achievable project had somehow been drawn out into a tight three year fit as a result of office politics, and lack of buy-in from certain countries. That had involved tight scrutiny, and hiring a new development team. Ultimately it was they who controlled the project. Kick-starting had worked, mercifully, and they had finally got the rollout back on track. But the cost overruns… You have to choose in the business world, as so often in life. It's either time or money. Tighter deadlines meant spending more.

But all that was now a fading memory. There was now a Support Team in place, and Trish had only taken one call since leaving. Free at last, but for how long? Projects were addictive, like beer to a drunk, and here she was slowly but surely seeking out another. The wait was never long, and demand for Project Managers invariably outweighed supply. You just rolled on from one position to the next, as she had been doing for years, starting out as a Business Analyst and growing into the Project Manager role. She was now 55 years old and wanted to go on for at least another five years. Early retirement and coffee mornings with friends? No thank you.

Trish called the agent an hour later. He seemed enthusiastic about the role. The company were looking to make an early decision, and get someone on board as soon as possible. A Skype interview would most likely be next week, and when confirmed, he would issue the company's details. All positive. She submitted her CV online, and emailed her two intended references. Both were soon acknowledged. So now just sit back and wait. It was January 20th.

Checking the websites for anything else produced nothing. It was, after all, January, the mid-winter lull after Christmas, and a time when company budgets were running low. There wasn't much around. She called a friend to check out a possible post but with only half interest: she was pinning her hopes on this retailing role.

The weekend came and went in unremarkable fashion. Some clothes shopping on Saturday afternoon was followed by a Sunday brunch at their local carvery. Trish was beginning to regret leaving the warmth of the Mediterranean for the cold, overcast weather of London. But you couldn't holiday for ever. Soon enough she would rejoin the rat race. Meanwhile there were several jobs at home to do, including some redecoration, which she intended to start the following day, hoping to finish before she was back in work.

Monday's job hunting brought up another opportunity, this time in Germany. Like most colleagues, Trish was reluctant to work away from home, having had enough of it in earlier life, but every post was worth an application, and she duly completed and returned the forms. Two in two days, a good start, and a feeling of unbounded optimism. She felt sure the interviewer for the retailing position would be back to the agent before the end of the week. Meanwhile press on with selecting paint for the spare bedroom, while there was time.

Wednesday and Thursday came and went with no calls either day. It was still early days but there was a negative feel. By Friday, she was back on the phone to the agent.

'Any news about the Project Manager role?' She asked.

'No, it's a strange one,' he replied, trying to remain optimistic in the face of nothing. 'I'm trying to track down the Head of IT. He wasn't there the last two days. It all seems to have gone quiet down there. You're still best placed of the candidates.'

She wasn't sure where 'down there' referred to. Geography was notoriously vague in job interviews to avoid recognition and hence a possible direct approach to the client. She knew it was the London area. The clue here suggested south. Could it be that

IT management were playing a waiting game? See who else came forward before starting interviews? Possibly, but why wait. Good candidates would be looking around and might find something else. If nothing had happened by this time next week, it was gone.

Meanwhile nothing else. Different agents she rang all commented on the time of year ('it never picks up until March'), as if that excused any lack of diligence on their part. The adverts were for other roles: web developers, functional analysts, system support. Usually Project Managers were less frequent, so no surprises. Sometimes you could cut through the red tape by approaching clients directly, but you had to know the client base well - who was spending money, what systems they ran, who to approach.

Waiting wasn't going to be easy, but she was still bullish.

The following Tuesday saw the end of that however. Peter Fleming, the agent, rang back. The retailing post had been withdrawn. The company had decided to source the role internally. At first she couldn't believe it. Why advertise it in the first place? Companies were essentially selfish, she concluded, and used every channel to source the right person even if they were only half serious, uncaring of the expectation level raised. So all that for nothing. Back to the drawing board.

Trish had still only been waiting two weeks for work. It had allowed her opportunity to paint the spare room, clear out some unwanted clothes and books, and spend time studying the latest IT press online. Things weren't desperate yet, and financially she could sustain a number of months out of work. That after all was life in the contract market. You were paid well but took risk. She was philosophical. And anyway, Ken was in full time work and they had his salary to live off.

A week later, a break arrived from a new recruitment agency. A company in Eindhoven, The Netherlands, was seeking two Project Managers for a major new warehouse system. The agency had contacted the company who were offering an immediate interview. This was promising indeed. Twenty four hours to prepare for imagined questions, study the company website, summarise her experience, and view the latest methodology developments. Trish worked hard as the 3pm Thursday deadline approached, her notes carefully organised, ready for this first round phone interview.

The hour arrived, no call from Mr. Dienkast of the company Project Office. She guessed they were running late, but the nerves were jangling. Any minute now... twelve past three, still no call. By twenty past, the nervousness was too much. She rang the agency, who promised to find out.

'They can't locate Mr. Dienkast, he's left for the day. They send their apologies.'

'So when is it to be rescheduled?'

'We'll need to get back to you.'

The trail had gone cold. There was a follow up call the next day, but only to say that a new appointment was being sought. Mr. Dienkast was still away, with no one certain as to his whereabouts. Strange.

Another opportunity to screw up into a paper ball and throw in the bin. All that preparation work for nothing. Hopes raised, only to be dashed. An apology was just inadequate. Trish felt that companies should pay interviewees to avoid time wasting. She had put in a day's work for nothing. They didn't care, it didn't affect them.

It was now February 10th. While she had been looking for work for less than a month, it was enough time to raise anxiety levels. The last time Trish had been out of work for any length of time was five years ago. Then it had been ten weeks. She had largely forgotten how it had felt at the time, but parts of that experience were coming back to her now. Depressing.

A weekend away with friends near Alfriston in Sussex restored Trish's perspective on life. It was only seven weeks after all since she had last worked. People her age were contemplating retirement, with probably a lower pension than hers would be. Why not do something completely different that involved less stress? Her working life to date had all been about cost-saving for the commercial world. She had impressive achievements, yes, but against a background of corporate culture. Her community or humanitarian work was non-existent. Why try that now, when a more comfortable life of retirement beckoned? But then why not? There was one cast-iron rod running through her body from top to toe, and that was the appetite for work. Give her a project, a mission, a goal, and she would chase it to the ends of the earth.

A Sunday roast in a sixteenth century inn, a walk up the South Downs in the fading late afternoon light, and a long chat about everything by a log fire, were the tonic Trish needed. It was good to be alive. You just needed to remind yourself of that. Since her friend, Beatrice, was retired, they could enjoy a leisurely Monday morning while the rest of the world sped off to work. Eventually Trish drove home, arriving at dusk. It felt as if she had been away two weeks.

Nothing of interest had come into her inbox, so the following day, with some reluctance, she restarted the whole process. Check the job sites, ring her contacts again, view social media. There was nothing. Ever the optimists, the recruitment agencies spoke hopefully of expected work but it was unconvincing. She even tried a new agency, strongly recommended by a friend, but the message was just the same: send us your CV and we'll keep you posted. She had already tried a couple of her previous managers, but while delighted to hear from her, neither had anything appropriate.

The redecoration and clearing out were complete, so it was 'what to do next' time She could fill two days looking at the new release of SMAP5, time well spent, but after that the options were running low. An afternoon call from an agent lifted her spirits. He had wind of something interesting, and would get back to her. Well at least it showed that there was some movement somewhere in the market. Ripples can travel a long way.

By Thursday she was exhausted with it all. February 22nd. It would be March in a week, and she had never dreamt it would take this long to get work. All her life she had been fortunate, as she now reflected. One job had led to another. Word of mouth, being in the right place at the right time, staying with the latest technology - it had all propelled her through a series of roles often with minimal breaks. And all had been challenging, the jobs she wanted, nothing second-best. She had amassed contacts over the years, but none were coming good now. It was just a bad time to look, and that wouldn't change till the new tax year in six weeks' time.

Was it worth looking for a six week assignment, even as a volunteer? Looking at those jobs, it meant either committing to a couple of hours a week, or working full time for at least three months, and Trish felt unable to do the latter. If offered the right professional role, she would be off, leaving volunteering behind. A matter of reality rather than selfishness. She eventually got interested in her local 'Friends' group, who were gardening at a local park once a week on a Friday morning. Anything to get out of the house. She could start tomorrow.

The first effort went well. She helped three others clearing dead leaves and branches from pathways. The taste of being busy again. Clearing, raking, bagging, putting full bags in the trailer. Bursts of energy interspersed with tea breaks from a thermos flask. Pity there wasn't more time available. It was enjoyable work, with much achieved, but paid for with sore muscles the next morning, she felt sure. It had also taken her mind off the job situation, and she could return home to focus on the weekend ahead.

Monday mornings – so disliked for being the end of the weekend, but doubly so if you wanted work and there was none around. While the nation went to work with purpose, you scratched around for something to do. However noble your intentions to study something, catch up with back reading or seek community-based work, the boredom was never far away. Some days, Trish didn't want to get out of bed. Nothing meant nothing. Either a job role would become available or you had to change your thinking. She had now given up on Project Manager roles and was focussing on Business Analyst openings, but it was something she hadn't done in over ten years. Even those were not in demand right now. Information Technology had always been the career to go for, with the lure of plenty of well paid jobs. But not for all, and not for ever.

Trish's other challenge was organisational. She had worked for years as an independent contractor with her own limited company. But now much Project Management expertise was either sought through a consultancy or from offshore. That might require her to return to a permanent role, which she was prepared to do. She had tried calling some consultancies and the conversations had been positive, but it was the same response as from the agents: we'll let you know. One of the problems with being out of work was that if you knew beforehand how long it was going to be, you would waste far less of your life worrying about it. It was the uncertainty that hurt. Something could turn up tomorrow and you'd be happy, but if not, it was indeed depressing. No one owed you a lucky break. You might wait forever, hanging on to the hope, till under the force of gravity it grew thin, snapped, and died. She was not there yet.

Thinking out of the box, Trish had contemplated changing career. At 55 years this would be a bold move, as all worthwhile careers required months if not years of training. She had often thought what she would like to become, what alternate career suited her, what indeed might be less high octane than her present one. Project Managers were invariably high pressured roles, feeling the force of both company management to keep costs down, and business users who wanted to expand scope and increase the workload. A case of trying to make something work and getting all to agree. There were times when Trish would have cheerfully quitted the profession, given the human element of the job, and having dealt with all manner of difficult individuals over the years. But perhaps she was too near retirement now to change horses.

Throughout this Ken had been great. Returning home regularly by 6pm, he brewed some coffee and talked to her about the day, always being a constant source of encouragement. It was he who had urged her to seek Business Analyst roles, and suggested she call the consultancies. He was her reality check, seeing the things she couldn't see for herself, even checking her CV for format and content. His message was clear: hang in there, something will give soon. Spring was in the air, and as the daylight lengthened and the days became warmer, so too did the belief that the wait would soon end.

Belief, self-confidence, that was the key to surviving this. Lose that and you'd impress no one at interview, however stunning your references and CV were. You had to practise that, to come over as confident at a time when it was draining out of you. Have your answers prepared, direct and factual with no waffle, spoken firmly with enthusiasm.

The week rolled on in expected fashion, no new opportunities, and no calls. Friday saw the start of March, and it was another fulfilling session at the park, this time weeding a stagnant pond. Life continued. Trish had looked at other voluntary roles including tutoring, but not having a teaching qualification was a problem for her. There was also the issue of DBS checks with the police because of working with children, and these could take some weeks.

It was there in the local paper, that she had initially put to one side, but now reread, a competition run by the Borough Council as part of Green Awareness week. How to create a carbon-free local environment. Cash prizes offered for the best three answers. Trish pondered. It was a subject dear to her heart: a greener country. Solar panels, wind farms, tidal and wave power. She firmly believed that there were many untapped sources of energy available, even commercially viable. Were she running the country, she would introduce a domestic carbon tax to be applied, like fuel excise duty, at the pump. Let those wanting or needing to travel pay for their emissions, with certain obvious social and health exemptions, and let's positively reward those who live a carbon-free existence, travelling by bicycle or electric car. In towns, she would introduce central zones where cars could not be driven, and the only available transport was from electric-powered or biofuel-powered buses. There would be capacity issues, as demand for such transport would exceed available power supply for the vehicles, but the challenge was to convert engines to handle biofuels, both for public and private transport. The carbon tax levied both on industry and domestic users would pay for much of this - unpopular no doubt, but necessary to tackle climate change and force households to go green. Rainwater collection and purification equipment would enable households to reduce reliance on mains water, and hence lower rainfall runoff in low lying areas. There were public health issues, of course, but all resolvable.

It was all highly ambitious, the world of 2050 not 2016, but achievable with commitment. Trish documented the steps, the changes in technology, society, and finance that would make all this possible. The days of the petrol-powered car were numbered. To produce enough ethanol, refining plant capacity would be vastly expanded, as also electric power points for cars and public transport. Cycle-only lanes would be set up around towns, based on the Dutch model, to encourage safe cycling. Public bike hire spots would be in place in all towns. Domestic rubbish burning anywhere would be banned and fined. Roof conversions, for both solar power and rainfall entrapment, would be required everywhere, subsidised from public funds. Individual wind turbines would be set up in unpopulated land areas to expand capacity.

Producing a plan was one thing, costing it another. There were so many unknowns, and so much uncosted technology, that the exercise was almost self-defeating. But it appealed to Trish's problem-solving mentality, and so she used technical drawing software to document the designs, and developed a costing model from that. It consumed two whole weeks at home, taking her mind firmly away from the job dilemma. She pieced together all the individual documents into an e-book, and submitted it to the Council. Like all green policy it was radical. You had to be radical to save the planet.

By mid-March, and with an early Easter looming the following week, Trish returned to the problem in hand. Maybe she could get a job as the Council's Green Advisor, she thought jokingly. All her work should lead somewhere.

How much intellectual property existed in the world, that had little or no commercial value? People who documented good ideas but had nowhere to put them, wrote good work but got no reward? The world of commercial work so often missed the important issues because there was no money in them. Ideas that never became patents and patents that never took off. There was money in repetition, not originality. Society needed to revalue its priorities, but who was to say what they were? With years of experience, Trish was better qualified to give value than ever before in her life, and had given excellent input to the Council's competition. Right now though, she was considered surplus in the marketplace, and of no current value.

She had become so busy that she had ignored her inbox. And there it was, a small Project Manager role for a dairy, sent from her preferred agent. Was she interested? She would call in the morning. Could this be it? Patience was a virtue.

WORKPLACE WOES

'Sorry, I know it's disgustingly late. Month-end reporting and all that.' Mike murmured his apology as he came through the door, knowing it would fall on deaf ears.

'Really, who is she?' Karen, his wife, replied sarcastically.

'Oh, don't you start. Come to the office and watch me if you like.' He hadn't expected a conciliatory response.

'No, I don't like. Really Mike, it's quarter to nine. Who else is back there? Just you I suppose?'

'Three others when I left. Pressure is on for all of us.'

'Sounds like you need to employ more people. Management stinginess again,' Karen sighed.

'Simple answer to a complex question. Anyway, any dinner?'

'In the oven. You'll need to reheat it.'

Mike Short was Head Accountant for the Sportswear Division at Actec Ltd, a wholesaler to popular High Street sports stores. Checking that all financial data had been uploaded, processed and final balances scrutinised was part of his monthly routine. Baltimore Head Office had little patience with delayed Corporate Income Statements (Form B12 in their parlance), and gave the narrowest of time slots for sending them. Errors and resubmissions were not tolerated. The need for accuracy meant careful checking.

But all that, however true, cut little ice at home. Karen, by contrast, was always one to leave work on time, and this was no exception in her current role as librarian at a local college. Work was work and finished at 5pm. Any time after that was unconditionally hers.

The demands of career and lifestyle were hard to balance. Mike knew that his occasional 11am starts at the office during non-peak times were never noticed since Karen was already at work. Salary in his case carried an expectation of some overtime. Everyone knew the score. This was a cut-throat business with small margins. You had to adapt quickly to changes in fashion, and catch the gym craze or parkrun bubble while it lasted. Bad months could be really bad. Three in a row and he would be needing a new job. The whole division would be restructured, and while accountants don't sell merchandise, the sweeping management changes would not spare him. No point in blaming anyone, success was everything.

He munched his overbaked cauliflower cheese, unsure what to say next. Perhaps nothing was the best policy. While there was little risk of marital rift, they lived in different worlds at work. At least Karen liked his company car, the one tangible thing from work that he could show her.

'Your mail is on the side table,' she broke the silence.

'Oh, OK. I'm sure it's all official.'

'Tomorrow night we're invited to Angela and Keith's for dinner. 7pm. Remember?'

He hadn't, and wasn't even sure that he had agreed to this engagement. Karen was being mischievous, knowing full well that he couldn't make it, but letting him suffer meanwhile.

'I really can't, dear. We're busy with all this till the end of the week.' Mike spoke in the vain hope that she would understand. At least perhaps his softer tone would appease her.

'So why did you agree to accept the invitation? You're making me look stupid going on my own, and we can't say no at this late stage. I'm sure Angela has bought the food already.' Karen was becoming visibly annoyed.

Mike couldn't very well say that he didn't remember accepting, so took the subsequent outburst on the nose. It would blow over, and the date would be rescheduled sometime soon, he felt sure.

Taking a phone call from one of her friends, Karen left the kitchen, leaving him in peace. The TV news held little interest for him, and the realisation that he was off schedule for the first time that day dawned on him. Lost for something to do, he opened the mail and then walked the dog, his mind elsewhere, travelling at a hundred miles per hour. It seemed hard to take a beating at work and then another at home afterwards, but that was life.

It was no use telling Karen that tomorrow night would be even worse. Having ultimate responsibility for the divisional figures involved him in a series of checks and counter checks. Confirming the ratio of cost of sales to sales revenue and so on. If any of these varied, investigations could take hours. Consolidating data could be a nightmare. It could be an 8pm finish if he was lucky, 10pm if unlucky. By Thursday it would start to ease, in theory at least. In practice he had two of his staff off sick and was having to roll his sleeves up. State of the art software could only do so much. You needed trained people to work it.

It really was a no-win situation, living through the pain. Next week would be different, easier. You just had to believe that.

And Karen… would she ever learn to be more understanding? It wasn't as if he was regularly away on business trips, or partying with his colleagues. The salary level justified the inconvenience. No pain no gain.

Mike fell asleep in the chair, waking at ten minutes to midnight and then making his way upstairs. The day which had started eighteen hours earlier was at last concluded. Tomorrow was another day.

He arrived at the office around 8.30am the following morning. Already it was a hive of activity, and he was quickly summoned to a management meeting, where the deadlines were impressed on everyone. This was the heaviest day, with two major and four supporting submissions to make to Baltimore.

There were issues with some of the data not reconciling, and with two staff off, an overflowing inbox and the phone ringing on a regular basis, Mike was tested to the limit. Getting temporary staff from inside or outside wasn't the solution. You had to know the accounting system to know where possible problems lay.

Lunchtime saw the immediate problems solved but there was a long way to go. The consolidations were redone and the reports regenerated. A long afternoon of checking was now in store to verify the figures. It had been a sub-average month, but that had been expected for October. November and December, with Christmas ahead, were the key ones.

It was painstaking work, ensuring all the costs were showing for each Distribution Centre. Thoroughness was the name of the game, and it always threw up areas to investigate, in this case payroll queries. Then there were the usual accruals and adjustments and a further reconsolidation to make. A point was reached where it seemed it would never be right.

Mike was dimly aware that it was now dark outside, and the office was emptying. The team worked well and stuck to the task. By 6pm, the first submission was ready, but soon became a problem. The corporate software was throwing up strange errors and none of their hard work would transmit. Calls to the US support line followed, with head-scratching on both sides, while the clock ticked away.

Mike poured his fifth coffee of the day. Ready to race but failed on a technicality. This was too much. An error that can be understood was fine, an obscure message with no online help, no good.

Eventually cross-checking revealed a missing balance and, fingers crossed, the submission worked and was received successfully. How everyone would have dearly loved to go home then, but there was more to do. Nothing was worse than being tired in the office, but still having to hang in there. It was 7.40pm.

'Pizza all round? Have you looked at the takeaway menu?' His Junior Accountant, Brian, was doing the rounds. A break was sorely needed.

Mike called home. This was looking like a 10pm exit. He knew full well that Karen would not have taken up the dinner invitation. He was greeted by a series of 'Hmmmmms' in the two minute conversation. Oh well, when you're in the doghouse...

The chat and jokes over a seafood pizza and cola gave way to the reluctant grind of preparing the second submission.

Brian had got it mostly done, but the detail needed checking. An hour later it had all worked, and they were locking the office up, fourteen hours after arriving.

After seeing everyone off, Mike turned the key in the ignition and drove home through the empty streets. It was 10.20pm. The house was in darkness, Karen having retired. It was just as well. Conversation would have been difficult, if not impossible. He checked on the dog and then tiptoed upstairs, his body tired, his mind in orbit. Sleep would be a while away as he lay on the bed thinking. It was exhausting. Was this all worth it, having most of the monthly stress packed into two days? How about looking for a job with a smoother load? Was Karen right? The problem with working for multinational companies... or was it worth tolerating it for the undeniably good money?

Anyway, for now the worst was over. It was downhill from here.

There is always the delusion that things will get better, that easier times are round the corner, that drudgery can give way and reveal its positive side. Such was the expectation of Mike and his team. Thursday would be the last tough day before some relaxation could set in.

And once the final two reports were sent by late afternoon, there was indeed a sense of optimism. The intense concentration required for these submissions gave way to a more carefree atmosphere. While the heat went up on the other divisions, Mike's team could bask in the warmth and relief of achievement.

However, there was still the bank reconciliation to perform, and as so often, the simpler tasks prove to be the most troublesome. Here, there were a number of unidentified entries on the statement that did not appear in their system. Investigation failed to help, and further information from the bank was required. Nothing was coming easily.

He was then called in to meet the IT team late afternoon. A software bug in one of the processes had caused incorrect currency reporting. Red faces all round, but fortunately no impact on the Baltimore reporting. Phewww!

He breathed a sigh of relief... but not for long.

'Mike, need to discuss something important.' Philip Dean, the Divisional Manager, ushered him into the office and closed the door.

'We've received a takeover bid from Sundown Sports. You know the size of their UK operation. It'll be hard to resist. They want to send a team in to view the last two years' accounts, starting Monday. I'm sure they'll give you a good grilling. Why this, why that and so on.'

'OK,' replied Mike, sighing inwardly. The easier first week of the month, he was hoping for, had just disappeared.

'Might mean some long days. You know how meticulous these guys can be. Like a tax audit.'

'Yes sure,' said Mike inwardly groaning. That was all too familiar from recent experience.

'You'll need the patience of Job. Best of luck. You'll manage. Book Meeting Room 1 for the duration.'

Mike walked back to his desk, trying to take it all in. More late nights. It was all happening.

Brian put his head round the door. 'Josie will be off another two weeks at least. Suspected glandular fever.'

'Oh heavens. More like a month I think with that. Really needed her here too.'

He sighed. Josie was a key member of his team. Losing her this month-end had been tough. Having her away while the takeover visit occurred would make it almost impossible to handle the day to day queries.

Oh well. Somehow they would cope. They always did. Half-dazed, he wandered over to the coffee machine. A double espresso was small consolation.

The office was proving particularly irritating today, and Mike felt like leaving before any more bad news could surface. The only consolation was that it was now 5.20pm and he was exiting at a decent hour. Home on time for once.

He switched off his laptop, retrieved his coat and made for the car park.

He walked in the door twenty minutes later.

'You're early,' said Karen with her usual wit.

'Have to come home sometime, you know how it is,' he replied laconically, quickly changing the subject, 'and how was your day?'

'Oh so so.' Whatever that meant.

Mike had learnt never to ask too much about his wife's job, suspecting that she had a general dislike of the workplace. Rarely would she say much. If work made character, she was the exception. Mike understood that many people don't like talking about their work, but you could be too extreme. We spend enough time working so why not discuss it?

'What's happening this weekend?' he asked, hoping that engaging her in conversation would heal the brokenness of the last two evenings.

'Well the Greens would like to hear from you. The invitation is now for Saturday.'

'Great, let's do it. Call them and accept.'

'OK,' she managed a brief smile. The atmosphere was beginning to thaw.

'And lunch at mum's on Sunday. So playing away twice,' she added.

'OK, good. So how about some Chinese food tonight? Save you cooking.'

'Sounds perfect.'

Domestic peace, still fragile, had once again returned.

CELESTIAL LESSONS

Sunlight streamed through the window of the small room in the university campus block as Ken McCready surveyed his new English tutorial group. After introductions from the four students, he tossed a topic into the ring, closely following the reaction.

'So which of these resemble most closely the journey of life: Walking, Running, Driving, or Flying?'

There was stunned silence for over a minute as the impact sunk in. Each grappled with the subject but didn't want to be the first to speak. A bit like being the first to jump off the diving board. It's ok, you go first.

Finally David spoke, 'It's all about the speed at which you want to live. Walking lets us see everything, and miss nothing. The slow lane, essential, but uninspiring.'

'That's why we need flying so that we can dream in the freedom of space,' added Richard, encouraged by the opener.

'You go over the same ground in a quicker and higher way, missing the detail for the big picture. Vision and mission thrive here. Once you have this, the walking becomes easier. The upper controls the lower.'

Helen's perceptive comments were noted by Ken, as keen to assess the group as to hear an answer.

'They are two extremes on two different wavelengths.'

'Space is also the place of faith, the vastness of God, however you perceive Him,' said David. 'And that itself is inspiration to keep our tired legs moving on the walk. You have a goal above the struggles.'

'Yes true, life as the testing ground. How you perform on earth conditions your place in the afterlife.'

Ken nodded. This group would not need much directing.

'And running?' He asked.

'Running is for those trying to make an impact: entrepreneurs, school builders, explorers, stretching the boundaries of life,' remarked Richard.

'Good, yes, yes,' Ken was becoming animated.

'Running need not be a race,' continued Richard, 'each runs at their own pace, but competes only with themselves, pacing themselves because life is a marathon not a sprint.'

'And you combine walking and running,' added Helen, 'but you can't combine the others. Flying doesn't go alongside driving. So the journey is really a walk-run.'

'What's that story?' said David. 'The tortoise and the hare. One runs and stops and falls asleep, while the other keeps plodding on consistently and wins. Something about life in that. Walkers can be winners.'

'Yes, yes, indeed. Good point. How about driving?' Ken steered the conversation to one side as if anxious to move on.

'Driving is about shelter and has no involvement with the environment. You are shielded from the weather, which is one of life's experiences, and go too fast to notice detail. It's not really about life, it's about speed and you, not others. Life should be about engaging with others.' Helen was becoming more prescriptive.

'OK what do the rest of you think?'

'Driving needs a road laid out. In life we all carve our own paths, rather than follow in others' footsteps. Each of us is different,' said Richard.

'So isn't flying worse? Flight paths? Even more extreme?' Ken interjected.

'Well yes,' said David, 'but we need it for inspiration, and you only get that in space. We need it to keep us going, otherwise the walking stuff doesn't happen.'

They all laughed. The group was growing in confidence.

'But…' Phyllis was making her first comment, 'we're taking this the wrong way round. I mean assuming that life is a journey. We should start with saying what is life?'

'True, yes, yes.' Ken's eyes lit up.

'It's a journey in time, so appears linear, from childhood to old age, but can also be a circle, like the four seasons over twelve months, or the same issues recurring. Deja vu and all that.'

'Like a spiral heading upwards.'

'Once you know what it is, you can work out the best mode of transport. Maybe a lift or escalator,' said Helen.

'Maybe there are breaks in the road, craters that we can't drive or run through. Disasters like flooding or fire. That's when we have to find an alternative way round.'

'What about stops? Places where you rest. We don't always have to move.' Phyllis was growing in confidence.

This was shaping well. The smile on Ken's face grew wider.

'Is life a road, a ditch, a stairway, a room, a beach or all of the above and more?'

'Oh don't complicate things!'

More laughter.

And so it went on, Ken analysing his new group, as they debated the issue, sharpening their minds accordingly. It led into an essay topic, their first termly assignment.

On the hour, they were done and the group dispersed. Richard and Helen headed for the coffee shop, a window of relaxation before their next lecture.

'Interesting topic. A bit off the wall,' she remarked.

'Yeah, some fun before the serious stuff, analysing eighteenth century poets and so on.'

'At least we can do the essay from our heads without having to read copious articles first.'

'More a case of what life isn't than what it is. Life has everything, is everything, but there must be something that it isn't,' mused Richard.

'You mean like walking along the bottom of the Pacific Ocean?'

'Yes, something like that. Take that away and we can do the rest.'

'Life is really like an explosion, it reaches everywhere. Our lives are so short compared to the millions of years of time, so each life is like a nano-second explosion.' Helen was in full flow.

'Absolutely… well you'll finish the essay in no time, but careful, I might pinch your ideas!'

Helen smiled and finished her coffee. It was time for her next lecture, while Richard was heading home.

'I'll do the practical first, some running. Make me feel like I've done some exercise.'

'Where do you run?' she asked.

'There's a route round the back of my flat, through the woods and round the park. Around three miles, takes about twenty five minutes. Three times a week. Keeps the mind active as well as the body.'

'Oh, OK. Good for you.'

He caught the bus home, changed into tee shirt and shorts, and knocked the old crusted mud from his running shoes. Resetting the timer on his watch, he set out. Recent wet weather had created soft mud, making safe footfall harder, but he soon picked up the track through the woods. The tree roots and jagged stones across his path could be the irritating issues and difficulties we all face. Filling up an application form, only to have it sent back because one answer was missing, dealing with excess noise from neighbours and so on. The twisting path symbolised an ability to adapt, find workarounds, respecting those problems but refusing to be beaten by them. Strength was everything.

Once out into the open fields, running became simpler, quicker, requiring less care and any trail was good. He enjoyed the breeze in his face, the children playing, and the sense of space. Life here was what you made it, no guidelines, any number of ways to your destination. A place for dreaming and thinking big. For some that was too much freedom; they needed the marked trail. For others it was sheer joy.

A gate at the end led to another, larger field. This was empty, overgrown, almost wild, yet so close to urban development. Richard ran quickly, happily, enjoying the feel of nature, but knowing that would soon change at the end where a main road crossed his path. From then on his route became a trail leading to an asphalted footpath, and a sense of being channelled and confined between fenced back gardens on either side. It lacked the feel good factor of the open fields, leaving a sense of mundaneness and blandness. The arteries of life so often sacrificed beauty for efficiency. But it got the job done and he could now turn left for the way home.

More woodland, as he ran over a carpet of fallen leaves, and then followed paths through the town park, climbing a hill and enjoying the view from the top, maybe a chance in life to see issues clearly with perspective. Reward for effort. He accelerated downhill and ran the few blocks back to the flat, making it home before the drizzling rain set in.

There is always a sense of satisfaction in completing a run, sprinting to the finish, but that too is often where the analogy with life ends. In life we don't know when the end will come, and we normally don't want to die. Runners frequently don't stop because they know how hard it is to get started again. There's also a sense of defeat in stopping and walking. But finishing is the goal, an end to exertion and with the satisfaction of doing a reasonable or even better time.

Richard could almost pinpoint his time to twenty five minutes and a few seconds. It never varied much as was the case today.

So, had he been too philosophical about this? A run was after all just a run, some exercise, not a reflection on the nature of life. If he had fallen or twisted his ankle, he might have had different feelings completely. What would he write in his essay? Was running perhaps the ultimate symbol of choice? You run because you can run. Once life removes choices, it becomes difficult and suffocating. Having restrictions, maybe poor health or old age, took those away. Choice meant freedom. To be free was to live. Keeping all options open meant the fullness of life. But it was also true that to be denied a choice was to appreciate those that you have.

To have walked the same route would have proved nothing. The movement comparisons, as in the group discussion, were inadequate. It was less a question of finding an analogy for life, of which there were plenty, than of seeing a best or better fit. Life is a progression yes, but not necessarily a journey to be travelled. It's multi-dimensional. Our lives move forward on different fronts, pushing on in one place and being forced back in another. Like an ever evolving shape, moving from long and thin to fat and square. That was a two dimensional view, but in reality it changed as a three dimensional mass, never stopping but ever changing slowly in shape, colour and texture. Maybe looking at a computer model was the answer. Forget the movement approach, go for the shape.

Richard pondered all this. He walked outside and looked at the clouds. Here perhaps was the best model of all. Right in front of our eyes, but rarely observed. Clouds move slowly, changing shape gradually in response to the atmospherics. Sometimes you could see faces, figures, ships, chariots, and as those shapes faded, others took over. Life is never the same today as yesterday. Time moves on, and the colour of a problem or opportunity changes from scarlet to a fading crimson, as it either loses importance or pushes itself to the forefront of our minds. Yesterday it floated towards us, today we catch and hold it, tomorrow it floats out of our world, soon to be forgotten. Blue cloudless sky or high altitude wisps of cirrus symbolised an easy life with no problems, whereas the build-up of cumulonimbus storm clouds represented big and overwhelming issues, only solved by the ensuing storm. Rain would fall, winds would blow, people would suffer, but it would pass and calmer times were ahead. Yes this was a better model, one that worked.

So there it was, painted on the biggest canvas life could provide, the sky. The rain had passed, and fluffy white happy clouds now drifted aimlessly by, unnoticed like the tide of life. Always there, changing by the minute, morphing from one form to a sweeter or sourer alternative. Sometimes successful, joyful, full, other times bitter, depressing, sad, or just plain dull and boring. You didn't need to move to see all this. Standing still or sitting down allowed perfect observation. Observation in turn led to insight. Each cloud pattern was different, just as each day was also unique.

Richard grabbed the pen. This could have been a primary school assignment but the task was timeless, for any age. His essay was in his head but needed to be written while his mental juices flowed. Now was the time.

THE LONG ROAD

'You will see a gate. Go through it into the field but stay to the right. The track follows a row of trees before descending to a stream. Take care when crossing.'

The monk smiled at her.

Sonia nodded and continued her journey. Her pace was slower now as the journey was long. On the way she had met other travellers, each preoccupied with their problems. Some had diverted and walked off into a wilderness, wandering without a clear plan. Others had stopped, sitting by the path in tears, lacking the will to continue. It was hard not to sympathise with their tales, but also important not to lose sight of one's own direction. Sometimes they cried for her to stay but she could not. To stop or go back risked failure.

Often, she wasn't sure herself. The path now ran through woodland and crossed a stream. It was so refreshing to feel the cool water in her hands, but the firm advice of the monks was not to drink it. She took off her sandals and dipped her tired feet in the water. It felt so good. Total immersion was on her mind, but a strong current near the far bank dissuaded her. Others had been swept downstream, even drowned- yet another of the traps along the way. Soon she would reach the small lodge, where she could rest on a firm mattress and cook the food provided by the monks. She would join them afterwards for prayer. They were kindly folk, charitable in nature, friendly in manner. If she worked lovingly to prepare food that was enough repayment.

Then there were those who didn't stop at the lodge, who thought they knew better and kept going, finding a ditch or old barn to sleep in. Walking at night was dangerous. Not only was there no light, but wild animals could be heard howling, casting fear into the bravest soul. A few travellers had ventured forth never to return, and all knew the risks. There was no medical help out here. The monks could wash and bandage wounds, but not fix broken legs or arms. Sonia had already passed some horrifically wounded people, lying dead or dying. There was no relief, just an agonising death. It was always best to stay indoors of a night.

The monks spoke about endurance. The journey was very long, even thousands of miles. She was just twenty two years old, but might be four times that age by the end. Her cloak and staff had to last the extremes of landscape and weather. She had already passed through the field of potholes, each so deep that you daren't fall down it. The ascent to the first mountain had proved tough too. The steep path had been never-ending or so it seemed, and in places jagged rocks replaced the smooth surface, slowing her progress to ensure she avoided hurting her feet. Yet further challenges lay ahead, notably the land of winter, noted for its Arctic temperature, and severe winds. Some had frozen to death there. Many had got lost as the path became snow-covered, visibility poor, and the way forward unclear.

Right now though, she was enjoying the cool breeze and freshness of the river valley, and duly arrived at the next lodge. She checked into the female dormitory, laying her cloak at the foot of the bed. Today had been a long walk of nearly thirty kilometres. Yes, that was thirty kilometres of experience that no one could remove, and thirty kilometres nearer her destination, but she had no idea how long this road would be. And it was important to keep to it, no matter what. Getting lost in the forest was a nightmare called madness. You could not find a way out and it drove you crazy, endlessly lost in the maze.

The resident monk got her to recount her day, each little incident remembered and discussed. It was a hard way to live, to have to learn a lesson from every moment of the day, but she was getting used to it and could see value in it. In this journey you needed every defence. She told him about the stream, the temptations and dangers of the current, but also the peaceful, soothing effect of running water. Nature the destroyer and the healer with the same feature, a fast flowing stream. She gave thanks to God for its beauty. Some days there was no relief from the heat and dust, made worse by the heavy cloak she had to wear. It was always a relief to rest on a bed at the lodge, the day's walking complete. There was often conversation to be had with a fellow traveller, experiences to be shared, warnings to be given. This might lead to them walking together the following day. The company was welcome, but Sonia knew not to rely on it, or let it delay her, as frequently they would travel at different speeds, making companionship impossible.

Life is a solo run. Even when married, we run our own race. Some are driven by ambition, running fast each day, but for how long? Others just want the joy of bringing up a family, finding happiness in a healthy home. Their pace is slower but consistent, the walk of those with an eye to the long term. Yet others are rudderless, with no clear plans or goals. They drift from the set path, getting lost in the woodland, and possibly never returning. Sonia knew the importance of self-reliance and motivation. Without those she would be lost. She had seen the price of failure, the pain and misery of quitting the path early.

But it took more than self-discipline to continue walking. She needed divine protection, something that didn't just drop from the sky but was built on by faith. Her own faith in God as a child had been neither strong nor encouraged by her family. As a teenager she had been curious to know more, but now, left to deal with life her own way, she saw the importance of faith. It was stronger than hope, and formed the basis of all her actions. It would be faith that pushed her onward day by day, and would provide a reward at the end of the road for her loyalty. She spoke of her faith with the monk at the lodge. He advised her to pray each night for guidance on the road as there were always unforeseen dangers, needing the quick thinking that arose from faith.

As she prepared the food and chatted to the only other traveller stopping the night, she reflected on how far she had come. Life had been good. Not easy but fulfilling. Difficulties borne by experience had brought strength and maturity. Wisdom had grown as only wisdom can, slowly but strongly. Sharing tales with others and learning of their experiences proved equally vital. Learning was everything.

After dinner shared between the three of them, Sonia cleared away and an hour later was asleep. The walking had left her physically tired, so that sleep came easily, and waking found her fresh and energised for the day ahead. Each day was unpredictable. There would be conversations with travellers, even pleas for help, places where the track got indistinct or split and she was unsure which branch to take. Her received advice was to keep to the right, so that is what she resolved to do. The breakfast and prayers at the lodge would prepare her physically, mentally, and spiritually for any difficulties. The key was to be always vigilant.

Next day she walked with Eunice, her fellow traveller, for some distance. Each carried a light pack. Inside it were a change of clothes, a water bottle, hat and some fruit. That was enough; you didn't need to be weighed down. The path was straight and flat, running beside a line of trees which gave some shade. Eunice's journey had been more troubled, and she had spent many fruitless nights in the wilderness. Worries over addiction and self-worth had almost finished her journey but, with advice from an old woman, she had picked herself up, found new purpose, and rejoined the main path. The monks at the lodges had been pleased to see her too, and she felt encouraged to move forward. Often the push you needed couldn't come from yourself; you needed others. Hearing of their experiences was helpful. Many had suffered diversions, so Eunice was not alone. Sonia was one of the fortunate ones.

They reached the first fork in the path, and with little discussion took to the right. It seemed a narrower, rockier option that trended uphill. Sometimes there would be an older man or woman to offer advice. They had taken the wrong turn in the past and returned to advise others, but you were fortunate to get such help. Usually you made your own choice and the difficulties experienced along one path could result in a return to the junction, and taking the other fork, humbled by experience. But deciding to return required strength and perception. Many blundered on in the belief that conditions could only get better. They didn't. They often got worse, and by then it was too late to return. You lived with your decision, albeit a mistake. In this case the wider left hand fork beckoned invitingly to a greener flatter landscape, with pink wildflowers breaking through the shrubs, but Sonia knew well that this would soon change and the track would turn into a muddy morass.

Walking around sharp crags required their staffs, and concentration on the twists and turns of the path. Climbing gave them a clear view of the terrain, and the hill ridges ahead of them. This was arid country with pale brownish grass giving way to bare sand and rock. They reached for their water bottles. Life was like this at times, empty, depressing, uninspiring. The sheer act of walking became difficult as each footfall had to be watched. And through all the sun beat down relentlessly, requiring them to cover their heads and keep to the little shade they could see.

Eunice did not respond well to the newer more difficult conditions. She slowed and stopped, leaving Sonia with the dilemma of whether to continue with her or not. While it might seem callous to leave her, this journey was not a Sunday afternoon walk in the park. Each person was ultimately responsible for themselves and being sucked into someone else's problems only brought you down. It was more important to keep going, after offering immediate help or advice. Sonia paused, ensured she had water, and suggested she lighten her load. They restarted but Eunice was finding it too difficult. Sonia stayed with her till they met an older woman who directed them to a nearby lodge. There, they parted company. Eunice walked to the lodge while Sonia set her eyes on the road ahead. She caught glimpses of the other track down below, lost in places in the mud, and was thankful to have made the right decision.

But it was tough and steep. Harder times brought out a tougher spirit in her. Her right foot hurt from landing on a jagged rock, but she continued onwards and upwards. She was nearing the summit when an old haggard monk appeared ahead.

'Greetings, traveller,' he said, his smile showing his missing teeth.

'Hello,' replied Sonia, now almost out of breath.

'You have done well to reach the top of Mount Hope. You have embraced difficulty and seen it through. Happier times and an easier path lie ahead, but beware that walking downhill can be as challenging as climbing. Watch your step, and don't rush. If you wish to give thanks first, we have a small chapel up here on the right.'

'Yes, I will.'

Giving thanks was important as Sonia, through earlier experience, had learned. We may think that we are guided by our own efforts, but these are of no use if not blessed by God. Being here at the summit was an event to give praise for. Looking back on the many who had stopped in pain, the many lost in the wildernesses, Sonia knew that few made it through and dependence on God was key. This was even more evident as conditions became progressively more difficult the further one went. She accepted the invitation readily, entered the small stone chapel and, sitting on the bench, meditated on the generosity of God. The monk seemed pleased, and with a knowing glance, wished her well for the way ahead, offering a few tips.

Sonia drew breath, preparing for the walk down and hopefully a lodge to stay in at the bottom. It was by now mid-afternoon. The monk had been right, walking downhill brought its own problems, so that in places she had to sit down and lift her legs over the rocks to safer footfall below. This was harsh, arid, unforgiving country, to be experienced slowly. The descent took time, but gradually the path straightened and widened and she could move more quickly. After another two miles, she met a younger man, Brian, and together they made for the nearest lodge.

Brian recounted his journey, which had started full of enthusiasm like Sonia's, but was now almost dying for cumulative tiredness and lack of energy. Some setbacks had deflated him and he lacked the will to recover. A bad experience with a girl who had left him, followed by job loss, was shown in the soft sinking mud of a wrong turn some days back. Unable to handle the anger, he had made his situation worse and sunk deeper before seeking help. Eventually he got a grip on himself, but found the necessary self discipline a heavy burden. Back on the path, his progress was consequently slow and laboured. Sonia tried to advise him to keep faith, one thing he seemed to lack. He would not be going much further without it. Some of the travellers found it hard to cope with the individual nature of this journey. Having faith gave you the inner strength to make it more bearable.

Dinner was a quiet affair, two monks sharing cheese, home baked bread and some apples from a nearby orchard - more a packed lunch than a sit down meal, but welcome nevertheless. She rinsed some clothes for the following day. In this heat they would be dry by morning. Then prayers with the assembled company. Sleep once again came quickly and fully, closing an absorbing day. Sonia just enjoyed lying on the bed, resting her weary legs. Climbing the mountain had been an event in itself.

Each day here saw movement. You could take rest days, indeed travel as slow as you wanted, or stop wherever you wanted, but the way was long and most wanted to press on while they could. Stopping happened when you had to stop - injured, unable to walk, lost, or you had mentally given up. The last was the most dangerous as there was no safety net, and you would be left to die. Walking by definition meant the will to walk. Lack that will and you cannot walk. There was no other form of transport here, just two legs. All were pilgrims on life's path. There were no airplanes to fly in, that could fast track the slow weeks. A day was twenty four hours long with walking for everyone. To travel far meant to travel steadily, to be happy with an even pace and not to strive or push for more. Dissatisfaction led to failure.

So what drove that resolve, the heart, the mind or both? It was a good question. Life required passion, energy and a desire to follow. These were of the heart. Yet it also took logic, thinking and care to avoid the pitfalls, all requiring an alert mind. And then there was faith in God built of the soul, for without that all the passion and care in the world would fail. It was easier to see the hand of God in this environment than in the physical fabric of life itself, the high street or the terraced houses. To be blessed was to move onward, to lack that was to miss the path.

Sonia pondered these many things along the way. She was a careful, hesitant girl, never one to test boundaries or indulge in extreme behaviour. She had curiosity, interest, and lacked any mental fatigue or cynicism. Her progress was steady, as required, with no time wasting diversions, and she respected the terrain and all advice given. The monks appreciated her approach. She was still young, and had many challenges ahead, but this girl, in their view, would succeed.

HAPPY NEW YEAR

'5…4…3…2.…1…Hooraaaay…Happy New Year!'

The sound of party poppers and the spray of champagne greeted the midnight hour. Another year gone, another to come. Coloured streamers descended from the ceiling onto the exuberant company.

'Yay, yay welcome 2016! Ooooooh! Goodbye 2015.'

Ellen smiled, she had never quite understood the need for such enthusiastic celebration as occurred at New Year. It seemed more about an excuse to celebrate than anything else. She too was glad to reach the milestone, but happy just to toast it quietly with friends. A wish for the future year given with a kind smile; the old year quietly closed and consigned to history.

She was attending a big gathering at the home of one of her colleagues.

'It's all about the past and the future,' said Ray, a friend's husband. 'Whether 2015 was a good or bad year for you doesn't matter. We're glad to see it go because we can't change it. 2016 sits like an artist's blank canvas, full of potential and possibilities. In a year's time those will all be used up and even if they were good experiences, we'll prefer to look at the future of 2017 than give thanks for a good 2016.'

'True, yes you're right. Never thought of it like that. 2016 could be a better year for you than 2017 when you look back, but before it starts 2017 feels better. New beats old,' agreed Ellen.

'Hey come on… help yourself to some champagne. Too much deep conversation over here.'

Fred, the host, wearing his party bowler hat, was doing the rounds, filling glasses, enjoying the moment. The TV showed fireworks over the River Thames and the numbers 2 0 1 6 lit up by laser beams over popular landmarks.

Noise broke out from a group in the corner, faces sprayed with champers, and glasses raised. Geoff, her husband, was in the middle of it all, she felt sure.

'So what will 2016 bring you, Ellen - a promotion, stock market windfall, holiday in the Caribbean?' asked Ray.

She smiled again. 'None of them, just some peace, for me, the family, country and the world. Not the answer you wanted eh?'

'2015 was a difficult year,' she continued. 'Mum died, Simon had to resit his entrance exam, the car accident, though thank goodness no one was badly hurt. Problems will always occur, but we just want the little ones this year. Please.'

'Yes indeed. You've had a bad run. Hope things improve. 2016 might be lucky. Digits add up to 9 which is positive in many cultures,' suggested Ray.

'You believe in that?'

'Not really... no year is any different from any other, whatever its numerical value and whether it marks the beginning, middle, or end of a decade. No superstitions for me.'

'Anyway, I'd better go and find Geoff. I'll hear him before I see him. The life and soul of the party.'

'OK then, see you soon.' Ray set off to join a group of his cricket mates.

The convivial mood continued, as his glass was filled, and the jokes flowed. Music was blasting from the TV as a rock band got into high gear. The room was awash with conversation and laughter. A-once-in-a-year-moment, full of optimism and goodwill.

'Well you know.'

'You know what? You've had too much to drink Alan, time to go home.'

'Rubbish, I'm not talking about how to grow marrows, but how to hold a dinner party: who to invite, seating arrangements, choice of wine, decorative entrees. You know all about that.'

The conversation in the study was switching topics fast.

'Oh, yes well… thank you. I just learnt it over time. Like to make people feel special. Love to entertain and all that. You see the best in people when they're relaxed.'

Vanessa was being polite. New Year was full of aimless, boorish monologues from men who had had too much to drink, and were trying a new line in conversation.

'We look forward to the first in 2016! Prawn salad and caviar.'

'You will be invited, rest assured.'

'To Vanessa, dinner parties and 2016.' He raised his glass.

'Really Alan, you're embarrassing me. Don't you have anything else to talk about?'

'Celebrate your talent!'

More toasts, more laughter.

'In Africa they go to church on New Years Eve. Everyone does for five to six hours, sometimes all night. They see in the New Year. Watchnight service they call it.'

'Really Church? No parties?'

Bill was addressing a group of friends. He had spent two years in Ghana, experiencing African culture as part of his role as an international school advisor.

'Yes, you see out the old year with God, thanking Him for your blessings, and see in the New Year with

Him too, asking for His protection over your family, job and so on.'

'Church on New Year's Eve. Sounds a bit boring. No champagne, no party, no fun.' Geoff was ever the celebrator.

'They don't think of it like that. It's not done to keep people away from alcohol and so on. They firmly believe that God controls their lives. If something happens in the future, it's by God's Grace. Some churches have their own prophets who can see future events and warn people of troubles ahead.'

'Prophets?'

'Yes, they have healing services. The prophet will facilitate God healing people in the service, provided they are ready to accept in faith.' Bill spoke sincerely. The difference in culture was never more marked than at New Year.

'Really?'

His small audience were quiet. Something they couldn't understand: the demonstrated power of healing.

'How long were you there?' asked Peter, as if to divert the intensity of the conversation.

'Just over two years. I had an apartment in Accra. Got to travel a bit. People were very welcoming. It's a lovely country.'

'Ever thought of going back?'

'Yes many times. Olive and I are thinking of doing a return visit later this year. We still have friends there. I'll be interested to see how much has changed, but in reality not much I think.'

'Must be interesting. Hope it works out. A goal for 2016,' said Peter politely.

The group nodded in agreement, somewhat stunned into silence.

'And he stood there when the ball came to him like a stunned mullet.'

'Ha ha ha ha.' The group dissolved into laughter as much with the impersonation as the words.

'But the funniest moment was when the goalkeeper dived to save the ball, missed it and crashed into Bruno. You know how big and fearsome he is. Goalkeeper murmured a weak apology and Bruno ran after him half way up the pitch. Referee had to intervene - forgot to award the penalty.'

A chorus of raucous laughter.

'More entertaining than the football I expect.'

'Indeed!'

'Referee then called six minutes of extra time and plays three. It really was a comedy of errors. Two yellows for their centre back and he stays on the pitch.'

'I guess you get one of those games every season. When will 2016's come?'

'Probably this Saturday. Tonbridge away. Never incident-free.'

'Oh dear.'

'Last year two serious injuries, a late controversial winning goal, and reluctant handshakes.'

'So this year has to be an improvement.'

'Don't count on it.'

3am. The company thinned, each couple making their farewells. The hard core stayed on for a while swapping stories. A few were slumped asleep on the sofas.

Geoff as ever was doing the rounds, wineglass in hand, introducing himself where he wasn't already known, and holding conversations that he wouldn't remember later.

Ellen managed a wry smile. She knew her husband so well. Her patience was his anchor. She sat down, joining a group discussion.

'New Year resolutions Ellen - come on now, I'm sure you have some?' asked Vanessa.

'Haven't given it a thought. Can always lose some weight, but tired of the gym. Just want some peace after last year.'

'Yeah sure, we could all do with better years I think. Be patient, it will happen.'

'Bob wants to retire soon so we could be having New Year 2017 on board a yacht in the Caribbean with any luck,' continued Vanessa wistfully.

'You wish.'

'Ha ha, you're right. I'm sure we'll still be here, freezing in the UK.'

'Waiting for Geoff eh?' Vanessa asked after a brief pause.

'Yes he always stays to the bitter end. Drag him away now and he's out of sorts all next day.'

4am was a good time to sneak home. Everyone had had something to drink but that was hours ago. Besides it was only a short distance, three miles round the back streets.

Geoff and Ellen were leaving the party, feeling the sobering effect of the cold air on their faces. She would happily have left two hours ago but waited till Geoff was finally done. She looked forward to sleeping in, having a lazy day ahead. How many people, looking back, could remember much about January 1st once the party was over?

He was obviously dead drunk, slurring his words. She thought about laying him in the back seat, but he somehow gathered the energy to sit in the front passenger seat and put a belt on.

2016, a chance to put 2015 behind them, to feel optimistic about life again. Move on from the problems that messed up your life. She felt free again. Who knows what it would bring, but hopefully a happier year. Some peace on a warm summer's evening, sipping wine in the pub garden, enjoying a laugh with friends. You had to dream. Life was dull without it.

Right now it was cold and the windows needed de-icing. Darkness was giving way to the pre-dawn greyness. There was no traffic around. She started the car and moved off, taking the familiar right and left turns, thinking of a nice lie-in minutes away. Simon should be home by now after an evening with his mates.

The route soon brought them to the junction with the main road, safely negotiated and with a mile to go she turned left through the housing estate. The roads were free, home was five minutes away. A tricky journey made easy at this time of day.

She turned right and then almost immediately left, where the road narrows with cars parked either side. The revelry was over, the streets quiet. She turned into the sharp bend, but saw the motor cyclist late, he must have been speeding, there was no way to avoid him… OH MY GOD!

You never think it will happen to you until it does.

ABOUT THE AUTHOR

Andrew Rees is from Bromley, south-east London but has spent time overseas in Australia (sixteen years), The Netherlands (five) and more recently Ghana (four). In Accra, Ghana he worked as a volunteer teacher and so became familiar with the lifestyle of an oburoni, but his career path has been in Information Technology for forty years. He has previously written 'Touchpoints' (2014, republished 2023) which also has twelve short stories, following on from 'Light Places' (2006) and 'Running Over' (2009). He lives in Cheltenham UK but returns to Ghana periodically.

Milton Keynes UK
Ingram Content Group UK Ltd.
UKHW010643290124
436892UK00001B/27

9 781962 497039